PUFFIN B

Anthony McGowan is a multi-award-winning author of
books for adults, teenagers and younger children. He has
a life-long obsession with the natural world, and has
travelled widely to study and observe it.

Books by Anthony McGowan

LEOPARD ADVENTURE

SHARK ADVENTURE

BEAR ADVENTURE

PYTHON ADVENTURE

PYTHON ADVENTURE

ANTHONY McGOWAN

Illustrated by Nelson Evergreen

PUFFIN

PUFFIN BOOKS

Published by the Penguin Group
Penguin Books Ltd, 80 Strand, London WC2R ORL, England
Penguin Group (USA) Inc., 375 Hudson Street, New York, New York 10014, USA
Penguin Group (Canada), 90 Eglinton Avenue East, Suite 700, Toronto, Ontario, Canada M4P 2Y3
(a division of Pearson Penguin Canada Inc.)
Penguin Ireland, 25 St Stephen's Green, Dublin 2, Ireland (a division of Penguin Books Ltd)
Penguin Group (Australia), 707 Collins Street, Melbourne, Victoria 3008, Australia
(a division of Pearson Australia Group Pty Ltd)
Penguin Books India Pvt Ltd, 11 Community Centre, Panchsheel Park, New Delhi – 110 017, India
Penguin Group (NZ), 67 Apollo Drive, Rosedale, Auckland 0632, New Zealand
(a division of Pearson New Zealand Ltd)
Penguin Books (South Africa) (Pty) Ltd, Block D, Rosebank Office Park,
181 Jan Smuts Avenue, Parktown North, Gauteng 2193, South Africa

Penguin Books Ltd, Registered Offices: 80 Strand, London WC2R ORL, England

www.puffinbooks.com

First published 2014
001

Text and illustrations copyright © Willard Price Literary Management Ltd, 2014
Map copyright © Puffin Books, 2014
Illustrations by Nelson Evergreen
All rights reserved

The moral right of the author and illustrator has been asserted

Set in 13/16pt Baskerville MT Std
Typeset by Jouve (UK), Milton Keynes
Printed in Great Britain by Clays Ltd, St Ives plc

British Library Cataloguing in Publication Data
A CIP catalogue record for this book is available from the British Library

ISBN: 978-0-141-33953-5

www.greenpenguin.co.uk

MIX
Paper from
responsible sources
FSC™ C018179

Penguin Books is committed to a sustainable
future for our business, our readers and our planet.
This book is made from Forest Stewardship
Council™ certified paper.

To all those fighting to protect our beautiful planet and the astounding and wondrous living things on it from the greed and stupidity of the rest of us

Acknowledgements

As ever, my thanks to Anthea Townsend, Samantha Mackintosh, Corinne Turner and Nelson Evergreen. Thanks also to Robert Twigger, whose magnificent book *Big Snake: The Hunt for the World's Longest Python* was a major source of inspiration and information.

Contents

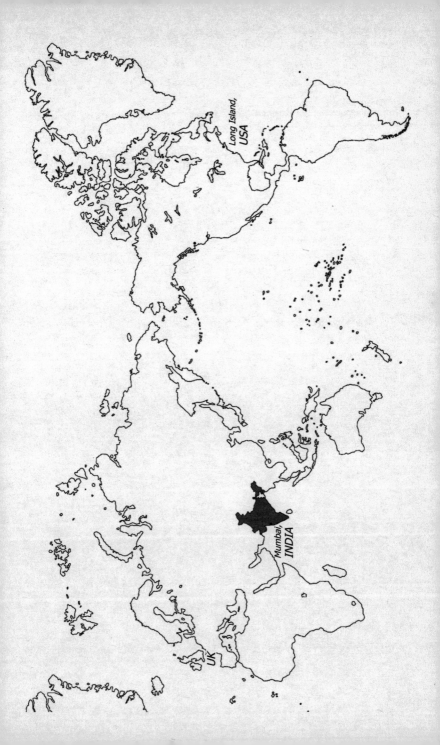

Part 1: Big Snake

Prelude

The old man was determined not to lose any more goats. He was sitting in the ancient baobab tree, its trunk so wide that it took six of the village children, holding hands with arms outstretched, to encircle it. He rested comfortably with his back against that huge trunk, and the village firearm – a battered shotgun that was even older than him – nestled in his lap.

The shotgun was an impressive-looking piece of machinery and, at close range – say within a couple of metres – it was still lethal. Beyond that, its wildly inaccurate spray of pellets would cover an area the size of a tennis court, making it very hard to inflict any real damage on man or beast. The bang, however, would be loud enough to wake the demons that dwelt atop the distant mountain that loomed up over the jungle. It was the bang, and not the pellets, that the old man was counting on to deter the goat thief.

And so in the tree he sat and waited. The goat – a nanny with lovely eyes, but a cantankerous temperament – was on the ground below him, tethered to a stake. She had nibbled at the dry grass for a while, bleated plaintively for the rest of the herd and then, content, it seemed, with the prospect of a night under the tree with the crazy old human in the branches above, she lay down and slept.

Every villager had a theory about who or what was taking the goats. To begin with, a leopard had been suspected. Some hotheads had even suggested a tiger may have come from the reserve at Buxa. But even the stealthiest tiger or leopard leaves pug marks, and none had been found.

Some of the men had suggested that it might be a pack of dhole – Indian wild dogs. Dhole were certainly bold and fearless predators, but they were rare now in this part of India and, besides, the one thing they were not was stealthy. They made no secret of their hunts, but simply chased down their prey with remorseless energy, communicating to each other all the while in unearthly whistles and screams.

No, had it been dhole, then the whole village would know of it, and every other living thing in the forest for miles around.

It pleased the old man to think that the goats were not being taken by dhole. They were not large creatures – hardly bigger than a jackal – and so death for their prey was slow, and to see, as he had done, a deer being eaten alive was not something he wished to recollect.

The old man had his own theory. The next village was several miles away and the people there were known to be untrustworthy. There was only one thing they could be relied upon for: that they would cheat at the annual cricket match between the two villages. The old man still distinctly remembered when, forty years before, he had been given out by a crooked umpire who was the father-in-law of the bowler.

So, yes, it was doubtless some young hooligan from the next village who was pilfering the goats. Well, the old man had no intention of shooting the scoundrel, but he would certainly give him a fright. And if it did turn out to be some leopard, perhaps one forced by old age or injury into preying on domestic animals, well then, he'd give that fellow a fright too.

And, thinking of this – of the leopard, and the scoundrels from the next village, and most of all about that long ago LBW decision, which he was sure had robbed him of a century and a permanent place in the folklore of his village – he fell asleep in the tree.

As he slumped there, propped comfortably against the great trunk, he was not aware of the huge shape that emerged from the low bushes. It was as thick around the middle as a big man, but longer, so much longer. It moved silently over the ground. This was not the careful watchfulness of a prey animal, nervous that it might be seen or heard by a hunter. No, this was the creeping stealth of a predator.

She approached the tree slowly and smoothly, as she had done a hundred times before. Her slitted reptilian eyes were intent upon the goat. But then the flickering tongue caught a taste of something interesting above in the branches, and she began to climb. Her long body wound easily round the massive trunk, and she crept silently through the foliage until she reached the spot, ten metres up, where the old man slept.

And the great snake paused.

She had eaten humans before. Young ones mainly. But the last was long ago. Her jaws could open wide, but those human shoulders were always a struggle. Down below, the goat promised to be a much easier morsel, slender enough to slip down without risking damaging her throat. And so she lowered herself – not bothering this time to slither down the trunk, but simply allowing her enormous body to dangle.

It was at just that moment that young Anand Narayan saw her as he came into the clearing, looking for his grandfather. He had been sent by his mother to bring the old man back for his dinner. It took Anand several seconds to understand the strange scene unfolding before his eyes. In that time he did what any young man might do – he reached for his mobile phone. The village had no running water other than the single tap outside the village shop, but the phone signal was good and strong. Anand pointed his phone at the snake and pressed the record button. And only then, the movie safely running, did he scream. This had two immediate effects.

Firstly, his scream startled the goat, which stood and bleated, and tried to pull away from the stake to which it was tethered. It could not see the snake, which hovered just above its head, but it could smell it, and this filled the little animal with terror. The scream did not disturb the snake, as snakes, although not deaf, have rather poor hearing, mainly limited to low-frequency vibrations – and Anand's hysterical shriek was very high-pitched indeed.

The second effect was that the old man jerked awake and fell out of the tree.

As he fell, he wailed and stretched out his hands, flailing in the air. There was, of course, nothing for him to grab on to. Except for the thick scaly body of the snake. The old man managed to get a hold of it without having the faintest idea what it was he grasped.

The snake held his weight for a moment or two,

but then lost its own grip on the branch above, and together the man and the snake landed on the ground next to the panicking goat.

This was not at all the easy meal that the snake had anticipated, and so, with a speed that belied her great size, she disappeared back into the forest, leaving both man and goat unconsumed.

Anand was already running to the aid of his grandfather who was emerging from a most peculiar dream. But the young fellow's thoughts were elsewhere. This, he knew, was going to look very good on YouTube.

The Party

Amazon Hunt was bored, agitated, annoyed and frustrated. Even if she'd had nothing else more important to occupy her mind, she was not made for small talk with millionaires or for hobnobbing with maharajas.

But there *was* something very much more important on her mind than raising money, even for a cause as good as TRACKS – the Trans-Regional Animal Conservation and Knowledge Society – an organization that she had joined recently in rather dramatic circumstances.

It was just a week since she had returned from the wilds of British Columbia, in Western Canada, where she had discovered the wreck of the light aircraft in which her parents, Roger and Ling-Mei Hunt, had been travelling. And carefully hidden on the site of the wreck she had also found her father's diary, which proved both that he was alive and that he was in possession of a secret that threatened the very existence of TRACKS.

The diary was badly burnt, and much of it was illegible, so Amazon's Uncle Hal had taken the diary off her to have it properly analysed by Dr Drexler, the TRACKS chief veterinary surgeon. Drexler had scanned each page of the diary, done what he could to enhance the images and returned a copy to Amazon. She kept the file on her iPad and felt that every moment she wasn't studying the burnt pages was wasted.

For now she was stuck on the roof terrace of a luxury apartment owned by an Indian financier called Pandu Singh with the TRACKS gang and dozens of important business people. The apartment was perched at the very top of a skyscraper – one of the tallest in Mumbai. Below, the city was spread out before her, speckled with countless lights like fallen stars, so that it seemed to mirror the night sky above.

Despite her frustration at being here, Amazon had to admit that the view was spectacular. Not even the sea away to the west was truly dark, for even there the lamps of solitary fishing boats bobbed, and yet more dazzling cascades of light spilled from the yachts of the millionaires out in the bay. The same millionaires that Amazon was now expected to charm and dazzle to raise money for TRACKS.

It was supposed to be something useful to do while

the experts were extracting whatever information could be gleaned from the burnt diary, but it still felt like torment to a young girl who wanted nothing more than to see her parents again.

Amazon sighed, sipped her 'cocktail' – a rather delicious mixture of exotic fruit juices – and smiled as another Mumbai entrepreneur told her about his new factory, which produced umbrellas, washing machines and electric pianos for the South-east Asian market.

Scattered around the gathering she spied various other members of TRACKS. There was dome-headed Dr Drexler, as stiff and formal as a tailor's dummy. Amazon felt another ripple of irritation. Just why wasn't he working on the diary? It was unbearable!

Her eye passed quickly on to Drexler's assistant. Miranda Coverdale was looking very pretty, Amazon had to concede, in a black cocktail dress. She was surrounded by a crowd of Mumbai industrialists, like flies around a honeypot. But Amazon knew that Miranda would have been more comfortable with a test tube and a Bunsen burner. She was no less dedicated to science than dry old Drexler.

Uncle Hal was working the room in a methodical way, shaking hands and smiling. He'd been doing this sort of thing for years, and he was good at it, but it was still a little like seeing a tiger pulling a plough.

Strangely, the one member of TRACKS who genuinely looked like he was enjoying himself was Bluey, the young Australian zoologist who had become a good friend to Amazon over the past couple of months. True, he was more used to shorts, T-shirt and flip-flops than the formal shirt and tie outfit he was sporting, but he had found a group of cricket-mad Indians to bond with, and they were laughing and joshing in the way that sports fans do. It looked to Amazon that a glass or two of beer had helped with the bonding process.

She looked around for her cousin, Frazer. He was probably up to no good, she thought, an involuntary smile twitching at the corners of her mouth.

'I don't know about you, but if I have to eat any more samosas or smile at any more millionaires I'm going to go mad. Shall we split?' Amazon jumped at the sound of Frazer's voice in her ear.

She turned to see her cousin standing right behind her. Like her, Frazer had been dressed up in smart clothes for the cocktail party. He had gelled back his hair, but now it looked like it was about to break loose, and the rest of him was sure to follow.

Amazon nodded gratefully. 'Let's go check out what the kids are up to.'

Back in the apartment was a games room full of technology: there was no games console, no electronic device so far devised by human ingenuity that wasn't present and correct in the room, along with white-leather easy chairs and retro beanbags perfect for lounging in.

It was the hang-out of Lakshmi and Arjuna, the teenage son and daughter of Pandu. They were sitting together on one of the beanbags, watching a video on Arjuna's mobile.

'Guys, you gotta see this,' said Lakshmi.

'What is it?' replied Frazer. 'If it's another cat that looks like Hitler or a duck on a skateboard, I'm going back out to join the oldsters on the roof to talk some more about stock options and share dividends. Then I'm going to jump into the ocean.'

'No, no,' laughed Arjuna, 'it's right up your street. Someone in Bengal in the east of India has taken a movie of the biggest snake ever beheld. It is a YouTube sensation. See, see!'

He held the phone out for Amazon and Frazer. And there was the movie taken by the boy in the village. The light was bad, and the movie grainy, but even so they could make out the unmistakable form of an enormous snake reaching down from the tree. And then came the almost comical sight of the old man falling, grabbing the snake and sliding harmlessly to the ground.

Amazon stared with open-mouthed astonishment.

'That must be a fake,' she said. 'Surely there aren't any snakes that big?'

'No, it is definitely real. You can see by the way it moves,' said Lakshmi.

'It sure looks real to me,' said Frazer. 'Where did you guys say the movie was filmed?'

'Bengal. In the jungle,' replied Arjuna. 'See – it's geotagged.'

Amazon was still stunned by the sheer size of the reptile. 'What kind of snake grows that long? A python of some kind . . .?'

Frazer nodded. 'You got it. They have Burmese pythons out there, but they usually only reach three or four metres. This thing is enormous. I reckon it's at least ten metres long. There're only two snakes in the world that grow to anything like that size: the anaconda, but it can't be one of those as they live in South America, and the –'

'Reticulated python,' cut in Amazon. 'I've just remembered – my dad once took me to see one in the reptile house in London Zoo. But that was only three metres long. This one must be the biggest snake in the world.'

Arjuna said, 'Well, it won't be the biggest snake in the world for much longer. The villagers will probably try to kill it to protect their livestock.'

Frazer nodded. 'And not just the animals. A reticulated python that size could easily tackle a human. And they're famous for being aggressive – most pythons are pretty shy and like to stay out of our way, but these guys like to rumble. And there's something else. This movie has gone round the world, hasn't it?'

'Oh yes,' said Lakshmi. 'It's all over the internet.'

'Well then, every professional wildlife collector in the world is going to be heading to that village, along with all kinds of cowboys and fortune-hunters. A snake that size is worth serious money. Dead or alive. And, even if they don't mean to kill it, capturing a seriously big snake is one of the great challenges in wildlife rescue, and there's a good chance the cowboys will do it some serious damage.'

'This is terrible!' said Amazon. 'We've got to find it first and get it to safety!'

'Dead right,' said Frazer. 'It's exactly what TRACKS is all about. We're gonna save that snake –'

'I thought I might find you lurking here,' came a voice from behind them. They swivelled to face Hal Hunt, Frazer's father. 'I know it's not the most exciting party in the history of the world, but, unless the money keeps rolling in, TRACKS is finished. Wait, what was that about a snake . . .?'

Frazer handed him the phone.

'Dad, we've got some *real* work to do.'

2
Amazon's Short Straw

It was the next day and Amazon Hunt's life had taken a definite turn for the worse. Rather than being in the jungle on an exciting race to reach the world's biggest snake before it was captured by a bunch of evil bounty hunters or slaughtered by frightened villagers, she was in an air-conditioned limousine on her way to the noisy, dusty city of Jaipur, where there would be more receptions, more meetings, more false smiles and, it was hoped, more cheques made out to TRACKS.

And it wasn't just that she craved the adventure – the search for the snake would have helped to give her some relief from the huge cloud of worry and anxiety about her parents . . .

She was travelling through the arid, baked and rather unlovely landscape of Rajasthan in northern India with Dr Drexler. Drexler himself looked arid and baked and rather unlovely in the unbearable heat, with his grey skin and wisps of grey hair around the bald dome of his head, and half-moon glasses perched on his nose as he read through some scientific report.

Amazon tried to read the title on the cover. *Considerations on the Changing pH Balance of the Indian Ocean, 1956–2007.*

Fascinating.

Amazon would have given anything to have joined Hal, Frazer, Bluey and Miranda as they had flown off in an executive jet belonging to one of the Mumbai millionaires. But Hal's logic had been, as ever, impeccable.

'I hate to do this to you, Amazon,' he'd said, 'but the truth is that Frazer, Bluey and I are the only ones who have gone after big snakes before. And we need Miranda to sedate it when we've caught it. If we had longer then I'd happily train you up too. But we don't have any time. For all we know there are already snake hunters out there now. Plus, the donors up in Jaipur will be disappointed about not meeting me, so it's vital to give them at least one member of the Hunt family. That's just the way things work out here.'

What went unspoken was the point that one of the reasons they needed the money was to continue the search for Amazon's mum and dad.

'We'll be back in three days max, anyway,' Hal had continued. 'Then I promise you'll get some time out from the fund-raising craziness. You can go and see the Asiatic lions out in the Gir Forest. TRACKS is helping with an operation to reintroduce them to a couple of other reserves in India. And,' he'd added, putting his hand on her shoulder, his tone softening, 'you never know – Doc Drexler may have managed by then to get some sense out of that burnt diary of Roger's. We know that someone found Roger and Ling-Mei, and took them away from the crash site by helicopter. Roger knew who was gunning for him. All we need is one clue from the diary, and we'll find them. That right, Doc?'

'Indeed,' Drexler had said. 'I have made some progress, using imaging technology I borrowed from a CIA, ah, acquaintance. It is able to pick up a trace of the chemical fingerprint left by the ink, even where the paper is almost completely carbonized, which is to say burnt. But it is a painstaking business, and rushing it could utterly destroy the paper . . . In any case, I, for one, am too old to be wrestling giant pythons, so I'll happily leave that to you, *ah*, adventurers. And it will be a pleasure to really get to know young Amazon.'

While Drexler looked through his report on ocean pH, Amazon read yet again the scans of the diary left by her father.

She had been so excited when Hal Hunt had found it, buried in the ashes of the campfire by the crashed aircraft in Canada. She had been sure that it would contain the answers to, well, *everything*. There was the terrible secret, some burning truth or scandal about TRACKS, that Roger had been coming to tell Hal. There was the wider plot of which it formed a part, something to do with animal welfare on a global scale. Most importantly, Amazon had been convinced that it would reveal who had captured her parents, and with that knowledge would come the even more important truth of where they were. Once they established that, then they could go about the last job: saving them.

And at first it seemed that the diary would give them the answers they needed. It began in a place she'd never even heard of – Kalmykia – a remote autonomous republic of the Russian Federation. It appeared as though her parents were there to help conserve an animal called the saiga – an antelope that had once ranged in herds counted in millions across the grasslands, but was now reduced by hunting and habitat loss to just a few thousand.

But, interspersed among the notes on saiga behaviour, there were references to a 'meeting with Sergei X' to 'discuss the issue at T'. 'T' must surely be TRACKS. 'Sergei is convinced that K's henchmen are on to him.'

The 'K' Amazon had learned about from Uncle Hal. He was Merlin Kaggs, an old enemy of Roger and Hal, going back to when they were just boys. He had been a low-grade conman, a murderer, a thief. More than once, he had tried to kill Roger and Hal, but every time he had come off second best. He had disappeared many years ago, but now seemed to have made a fortune during the chaotic time after the collapse of the Soviet Union. He had reinvented himself as an oligarch – one of the billionaires who held so much power and influence in Russia.

There were more pages about the saiga, and then this:

There is now no doubt. The saiga are not being killed by local hunters. The herds are being depleted, yet there is no evidence of shooting, no carcasses, no blood. Ling-Mei's theory had been that what lay behind all this was the use of saiga horns in Chinese traditional medicine, where they are occasionally used as a substitute for rhino horn. But in that case we would find the bodies with the horns removed – the killers would have no use for the rest of the animal. The only conclusion we can draw is that the animals are being captured alive, and taken to . . .

Frustratingly, here the page had been too badly burnt to read. There was just the singed paper, gradually turning blacker towards the bottom.

The parts that most moved Amazon were the sections – short but so, so sweet – where her parents mentioned her.

'We miss our little Amazon so much. Ling-Mei was very upset last night. She said that in future we could not leave our daughter behind. Either we travel only in the school holidays or we take her out of school and bring her with us, taking a tutor along or teaching her ourselves. Neither of us can bear these absences any longer. A little girl needs her mom and dad. And a mom and dad need their little girl.

Strangely, the pages with these kinds of personal comments about her, or those in which Roger spoke of his sadness about the breach with his brother Hal, were, although singed, still readable. It was as though a guardian angel had watched over the pages written with love . . . It was the ones that dealt with the meaty issues – who was betraying TRACKS, why they were doing it and where the animals were being sent – that had been destroyed.

3
Comfort Break

Still the limousine drove on through countryside as dry and brown as the diary of Roger Hunt. Having warned her several times that the battery was low, Amazon's iPad finally ran out of juice and turned itself off.

'I need a comfort break,' said Dr Drexler, interrupting the long silence of the trip.

He tapped on the window separating the passenger seats from the driver, and pointed towards an approaching roadside café. The car pulled in. Amazon opened the door and was hit by a wave of heat that had an almost physical force. Suddenly the air-conditioned car seemed like a very nice place to be.

'I'm staying in the car,' she said to Drexler.

'As you choose,' he replied, his mouth a narrow line of disapproval, and disappeared into the scruffy and cheerless interior of the café.

Somehow it was always easier to breathe when Dr Drexler wasn't around, but now Amazon was

seriously bored. The countryside had been mono-
tonous, but at least it had changed, slowly. Now there
was nothing to look at. Her laptop was locked in the
boot, as were the books she had brought with her.
Anyway, all she really wanted to read was her father's
diary.

Then she saw Dr Drexler's laptop on the floor of
the car, poking out from under his seat. She knew
that he had the PDF of the diary on there. She felt
a little guilty about opening someone else's laptop,
but not so guilty that it stopped her from doing it.

It asked for a password. She knew that all of the
TRACKS computers had the same password:
SEMITA (which was Latin for TRACKS), followed
by the initials of the user. What on earth was
Dr Drexler's first name, she wondered?

David? Something boring like that. No, John, that
was it. Amazon typed SEMITAJD and was in. She
did a quick search for 'Roger Hunt's Diary' and
found the file. She double-clicked on it and it opened
up in Adobe Reader.

The bigger screen of the laptop made it much
easier to read Roger's spidery handwriting, and the
file seemed to be of higher resolution than the one
she had on her iPad – she was even able to make out
an extra word or two under the scorched parts.
Nothing that made much sense, out of context, but
at least it gave her some hope.

But then she had another pang of conscience

about Drexler's laptop. No, conscience wasn't quite the right word. Amazon didn't actually think there was anything morally wrong about what she was doing, but she still didn't want him to know that she had done it. TRACKS' head of science was a private man, and she didn't think he'd appreciate anyone prying into his affairs, even innocently. However, she had a solution.

She fished in the backpack at her feet and pulled out a USB stick. It had a couple of downloaded movies on it, but there was enough room for one small file. She dragged the PDF file to the USB drive icon. To her surprise a message came up saying that there wasn't enough room. She tutted, trashed one of the movies and this time the copying worked. She slipped the USB stick back into her pocket, closed up the laptop and replaced it under the seat.

A minute or two later, Dr Drexler came back.

'Quite shocking,' he said as he made himself comfortable again in the cool of the car, 'the state of public conveniences in this country. I had to give a hundred rupees each to two fellows in there, and you'd think the least they could do would be to . . . well, anyway, things will be rather different when we arrive at the Maharaja of Jaipod's residence.'

'What's it like?' asked Amazon, relieved that Drexler hadn't noticed anything amiss with his laptop.

'Oh, a palace, quite definitely a palace. The largest

in Rajasthan, in fact. And, as you know, the Maharaja also owns a huge estate further south, which he has turned into the biggest privately owned game reserve in India. TRACKS have been sending rescued animals to him for several years now, for, ah, *rehabilitation*, if that's the word.'

'Is that the guy with the Asiatic lions? Uncle Hal mentioned him to me.'

'Yes, yes. In fact, his reserve is the only place in the world where you can see lions and tigers together in the wild, although of course they stick to their own preferred habitats. And of course there are leopards, the dhole – that's the Indian wild dog – a fierce predator in its own right. And in the rivers there are mugger crocodiles – the biggest in India . . .'

'Sounds quite a place. I'd love to see it.'

'Oh, I'm sure you will, one day.'

4

The Love of the Hunt

Frazer's journey could not have been more different. He was loving every second of it: the screeching drive to the private runway at the edge of Mumbai international airport; the sleek little executive jet with leather seats and, if he'd wanted it, champagne on ice (he settled for iced tea); the chance to talk with his dad about the adventures they'd shared, as well as the ones Hal and Roger had been on at Frazer's age.

Hal himself was clearly relieved to be away from the fund-raising side of things and back to the thrill of actually saving animals. But there was one thing killing the joy for both of them.

'Hope Amazon isn't too bored,' said Frazer.

His father sighed. 'Me too. Drex is a good man and a fine scientist, but he can be a dry old stick. Not really the sort of company you'd choose for a young girl. It's a shame we couldn't have left Miranda behind as well . . .'

Frazer pulled a face. In his mind Miranda was

almost as dry a stick as Dr Drexler. Then he realized that his father's comments could have been taken in two ways, and that made him grin.

'I'm not deaf, you know,' came Miranda's voice from behind them. 'Or blind. I can see your face reflected in the window.'

Hal and Frazer looked at each other and pulled the same naughty schoolboy face. Frazer hadn't seen his dad looking so relaxed in a long time.

'You love this, don't you, Dad?' he said.

'You mean flying around in private jets?'

'I mean saving animals. Rescuing giant snakes. Jungles. Deserts. The works.'

'Guess you got me, son.'

'And you know what, Dad?' Frazer replied.

'I think I do, Fraze. Yep, I think I do.'

And the look they exchanged meant that Frazer didn't have to say that he loved it too.

5

The Maharaja's Pleasure Dome

Dr Drexler hadn't been joking about the palace. Amazon knew that they were going to be attending a banquet there, but she had assumed that they'd be stopping at a hotel first, to freshen up. But it became clear as the palace came into view, and gradually filled her vision, that they were going directly there.

'Yes, my dear,' said Dr Drexler, as if reading her mind, 'we will be staying in the palace while we are in Jaipur. Unlike the other business people and financiers and politicians you have met so far in Mumbai and Delhi, you are not primarily here to charm your way into bank accounts and wallets. The Maharaja is an old, old friend of TRACKS and, indeed, of mine.'

Amazon was a little surprised. 'OK, what *am* I here for?'

'You are here, my dear, as a reward for the Maharaja.'

Amazon didn't much like the sound of that.

'You make me sound like an ice cream given to some kid for being good.'

Drexler looked blank for a moment, and then emitted his dry, mirthless laugh.

'Not at all, dear child. It is just that the Maharaja was educated at a public school in England and consequently loves all things English. He simply wants to talk with you about English country meadows and bluebell woods and the like.'

When Amazon next looked up, except for the tip of the gleaming dome, the palace was no longer visible. It was obscured by a high wall.

The car drove through a mighty gateway, lacking only a portcullis to complete the picture. On either side of the gateway there stood a pure white horse with flowing mane and tail. Each horse had a tall, handsome rider, sporting a plumed turban and a moustache that looked like some extraordinary creature TRACKS would take an interest in. These two magnificent warriors saluted them with drawn sabres.

'Are they for real?' asked an astonished Amazon.

'Oh yes, very much so. The guard is both ceremonial and practical. The Maharaja is a great man and, like all great men, he has many enemies.'

Once through the gateway, the palace came back into view. From a distance it had a delicate and dreamlike beauty. At close range the sense of light and grace was replaced by something graver,

31

weightier, more magisterial. It was a truly awe-inspiring structure with a great dome like that of St Paul's Cathedral in the middle, and a tall, thin tower, topped with a slender, onion-shaped dome, at each corner. The walls were of a marble of such dazzling whiteness that it genuinely hurt Amazon's eyes to gaze upon it.

But even the white marble seemed dull in comparison to the dome.

'That's not really made of –'

'Gold? No, my dear. Merely burnished copper. But yes, it is magnificent, isn't it? It is said to be visible from space as a pool of molten gold, as if a new sun were being born, right here in Rajasthan.'

Amazon had never heard Drexler speak like this, and she found it a little disconcerting.

'So you've been here before?' she asked.

'Oh yes, many times. You see, the Maharaja is my godfather. He was at school with my father and has helped me all my life. He paid my school fees. It is not an exaggeration to say that I owe everything I have achieved to him.'

By now the car, crunching along the gravel drive, had almost reached the palace itself. A reception committee was awaiting them. There were servants in elaborate uniforms, looking like something from a theatrical performance. Next to them stood the most bizarre band of musicians Amazon had ever seen: some held traditional Indian instruments, such as sitars, pungis and pulluvan pattus, while others were equipped with bagpipes, trombones, bugles and drums.

As soon as the car drew up before them, the band struck up. It sounded, to Amazon, as though every member were playing a different tune, such was the cacophony. She thought that it was probably just Indian music, and she was being ignorant. But then an argument broke out between several of the band members, followed by apparent agreement. The band started up again and what they played was clearly supposed to be 'God Save the Queen'.

'Smile, my dear,' said Drexler. 'This is all in your honour.'

Never mind smiling: Amazon was finding it difficult not to laugh.

An ancient lady, who looked almost like a few handfuls of the dry earth formed into the shape of a person, dipped her thumb into a pot of powdery red dye and then anointed both of them on the forehead. An equally old man next to her then pushed a few broken grains of rice into the red spot.

'This is called the bindi,' said Drexler. 'It is a blessing, for luck. And it will protect you from demons and suchlike.'

And then a very grand figure approached them.

'Is this the Maharaja?' Amazon asked Dr Drexler out of the side of her mouth.

'Oh dear, no, not at all,' he chortled.

'Please to follow,' said the man, giving a little bow.

He led them through the main doors of the palace. They were made from thick wood, covered by bronze panels showing intricate scenes of battles from bygone times. At a height that Amazon would have had to jump to reach there was a line of vicious spikes sticking out. Dr Drexler saw her gazing at them.

'To deter elephants,' he said, his normally tight mouth giving way to a grim little smile. 'Any elephant rash enough to try to barge the door down would find its brain impaled upon a spike.'

Amazon couldn't help but cry out in distress. 'Oh, but that's not fair! The poor elephants! It wasn't their fault . . .'

'Those were cruel times,' said Drexler. 'Very cruel. Anyway, let's put those thoughts out of *our* heads. We are here to charm and delight the Maharaja, remember. He has given millions to our projects, as well as supporting his own sanctuary.'

The grave and grand servant passed them on to another, a little less grand, who showed them silently to their rooms. At his door Drexler said, 'We'll be dining with the Maharaja at seven. Do try to look . . .'

'I'll do my best,' replied Amazon, although all she had were her usual neat and unfussy clothes.

The servant then led Amazon to her room. It was like a mini palace in itself. There were, in fact, three rooms. First a lovely drawing room with antique

34

furniture carved into complex patterns, and wall hangings showing gardens full of pretty girls, handsome warriors, proud peacocks, glittering pheasants, big-eyed antelope and fierce tigers.

An arch led through to her bedroom, in the middle of which was the sort of fairy-tale princess bed she'd always scorned as totally STUPID; but now that she saw it, in all its glory, she couldn't help but burst into joyous laughter. She ran and hurled herself on to it. And sank so deeply it was as if the mattress were made from clouds and spider silk.

The bathroom appeared almost to have been carved from a single giant block of marble. The bath itself was huge and square, and Amazon reckoned she could do a couple of strokes of front crawl before she cracked her head on the edge. The taps were gold.

'Tacky,' she said to herself. And then she realized that the silent servant was still there, looking at her with humble submissiveness.

'Oh, sorry . . .' said Amazon, looking for some rupees to give him.

Suddenly his faced changed to a look of horror – in fact, it was close to terror. He shook his head wildly.

'OK, no tip, I get it,' said a startled Amazon. 'But, er, can't you speak English?'

The man nodded slightly, and then pointed to his mouth, and shook his head.

'Oh, I see, you can understand English but not speak it?'

He nodded.

'And I guess you just wanted to know if there was anything else I needed?'

The man nodded. But there was something about his manner that made Amazon think that he did, in fact, want to communicate something to her. But, whatever it was, he failed, and so turned away after another short bow, leaving her to enjoy the luxury.

'I so wish Frazer was here to see this,' she sighed. Yes, how much more fun it would be if her cousin were there to laugh about it with.

But then another thought crowded that one out. No, of course it wouldn't be fun unless her parents were safe.

6

Jungle Drive

Although Frazer's journey had begun well, it soon changed, once that fun flight was over and the little aircraft had touched down on a rough airstrip that really wasn't designed for jets – even those as light and nimble as this one.

A jeep was waiting for them by the runway when they emerged from the plane. Frazer soon found out that it had been sent by a local police inspector who had known Hal Hunt when he was a boy.

'How long to get to the village?' Hal asked the driver.

The man smiled, moved his head from side to side in the characteristic Indian way and said, 'Oh, soon, very soon.'

'Very soon' turned out to mean five hours spent driving on roads that began as potholed death traps and steadily became worse, until they were on tracks that were barely distinguishable from the jungle around them. Twice they got stuck in quagmires, which involved all the adults pushing while Frazer, the lightest, drove, working the gears to try to find some traction. When they did manage to get moving, Frazer, despite the fact that he was used to travelling rough, felt seasick, so much did the jeep lurch up and down and from side to side.

It was also incredibly hot and sticky, and the agonizingly slow speed meant that they never managed to get a decent breeze to pass through the windows.

They drove through a series of villages, each one more ragged and ramshackle than the last. They were often greeted by laughing children, who followed the jeep, begging for money through the windows. Good-natured Bluey could not resist the smiles, and he had soon given away all his spare cash.

Their progress through the villages was further slowed by the domestic animals that wandered around, completely, as far as Frazer could tell, at liberty. Scraggy goats, rather elegant white cows, hairy black pigs and lumbering water buffalo ambled along or squatted in the middle of the track.

As the gaps between the villages increased, so the landscape gradually became less cultivated: the paddy fields of rice grew smaller and the patches of woodland thicker.

Finally, an hour beyond the last settlement and now deep in the forest, they came to the village where the python had been filmed.

As usual, the village children – alerted by the grinding of the jeep engine as it struggled along the rutted path – were the first to appear, smiling and laughing.

The driver pulled up outside a hut a little larger than the others.

'Headman,' he explained, as they all piled out of the jeep.

There followed a rather hectic half-hour, during which Hal, speaking a mixture of English and Hindi, first tried to explain to the headman of the village – a rather self-important chap with a bulging stomach and unfeasibly hairy ears – who he was and why the Trackers were there. By the time he had finished talking to him, a surprisingly large crowd had gathered round them.

Soon, as word spread that the circus was in town, ancient puttering motorbikes began to arrive, often loaded precariously with whole families – father, mother, grandfather, grandmother, two or three grandchildren, arranged like a human pyramid.

Alongside the people came chattering monkeys, curious to see what food might be available from the crowds. Frazer was annoyed to note that they were rhesus macaques, their pink, very human faces bearing their usual sly, shifty appearance, as if they'd been caught doing something shameful. Actually, Frazer knew that he was being a little unfair – a bold macaque had stolen a candy bar from him in Mumbai, and he had found it difficult to forgive the whole species.

He was much fonder of the grey langurs. To Frazer's eye, these monkeys had a more graceful air about them. He thought their wrinkled black faces carried a serious, respectable expression. They moved with a lovely liquid stride, like grey water flowing over the land. But here in the village it was all macaques, and they scowled back at him, no doubt sensing and reflecting back his own dislike.

And then the headman clapped his hands and barked an order for the old man who had started the rumpus to be brought before him.

'While we're hanging around,' said Hal to Frazer, 'why don't you give Amazon a call and see how she's getting on?'

'Sure,' said Frazer. He took the phone from his pocket, but before he could hit Amazon's number a particularly bold macaque swooped down from one of the rooftops and snatched it.

'HEY!' yelled Frazer, trying to grab the phone back. 'That's mine!'

But it was too late. The monkey was already swinging away through the trees with its shiny new toy.

Frazer heard a laugh and saw Bluey doubled up. 'He's probably just going to check his apebook page,' the Aussie grinned.

Frazer also saw the much sterner face of his father.

'Yeah, I know,' Frazer said, his shoulders slumping, 'that's coming out of my allowance.'

7

Burnt Offerings

Alone in her palatial room, Amazon perused the new higher definition images of the journal on her laptop. Excited to begin with, her heart sank as she scrolled through the first few pages of the document. She'd hoped to be able to zoom in on some of the burnt sections and perhaps make out more of the words. But it was no use. She had discovered that a blackened piece of paper looks more or less the same from close up as from far away. She also wasn't used to Adobe Acrobat. It seemed like an unnecessarily complicated piece of software for just looking at documents.

She started to go through the menus at the top of the screen, just to see what they did. A couple of idle clicks took her to the View menu, where she'd already found the way to zoom in on the page, and then on to an option that said Show/Hide. Amazon clicked on that and found more meaningless options, most of which did very little that was useful to her. Then she clicked on Layers. The page in front of her changed. The diary page was still there – charred beyond recognition – but to the left-hand side a panel had popped up. The panel was divided into four boxes. In each box was a title:

burn1
burn2
page curl
distress.

Next to each was a little icon of a padlock. Except for the one that said 'distress'. That had an icon of an eye next to it. She clicked burn1, burn2 and page curl. Nothing happened. Then, still not really thinking – in fact, her mind was more on the dinner she was shortly to have, and what on earth to wear – she moved the cursor over the 'distress' box and clicked. Instantly, the page of the diary she was looking at changed. The scanned paper became whiter and the writing at the top of the page clearer.

Suddenly Amazon was fully focused on the screen once again.

She tried to remember the ICT classes she had taken back at her boarding school in England. They'd had one lesson on Photoshop, which had the same layer thingies. Her fingers remembered what to do before her brain was conscious of it. She right-clicked the padlock icon next to 'page curl'. A box popped up offering her two options – 'show layer' and 'properties'. She clicked on 'properties'. Now she was in a box with more options. Her eyes darted around until she found a small box labelled 'lock' with a tick in it. She clicked on the tick, which cleared it. Next, she clicked 'OK' and was back on the main page, with the diary. The lock had turned into an eye.

And now she felt a growing excitement. She knew that this all meant something, but her mind could not quite yet put the pieces together.

Now, when she clicked on it, the bottom of the page, which had appeared to have curled as it burned, was simply black. In a flash she realized that the curling effect had been added. So, her fingers moving with robotic speed, she repeated the process for the burn1 and burn2 layers.

Suddenly Amazon found herself gazing at a perfectly legible page. The very bottom of it was still black from the genuine fire in which her Uncle Hal had found it, but the words were all there. She read feverishly. Then she clicked on the next page and began again.

By the time she had finished, Amazon could hardly breathe. Slowly she moved the mouse to hover over the File Properties dialogue box. She knew now that this is where she should have started all along – where she could find the identity of the person who had tampered with the files.

And there, in black and white, she saw the author

of the document, the person who must have made these changes, obscuring and hiding the plain truth that lay beneath.

It was not what Amazon had expected. In fact, it hit her like a punch in the stomach.

The name she read was: MIRANDA COVERDALE.

8

The Snake Hunt Begins

Eventually, the old man who had fallen from the tree was found, along with Anand, the grandson who had captured it all on his phone. Both seemed very happy to be the centre of attention.

'Can you take us to where all this happened?' Hal asked.

Anand replied in excellent English: 'Oh yes. Follow me.'

The whole village, plus every other living person from miles around, along with a good number of the village macaques, now trailed out to the baobab tree in the clearing.

Frazer overheard Miranda Coverdale saying to Hal, 'This is hopeless. How are we supposed to work with all these . . . *civilians* in the way?'

'Miranda,' replied Hal, 'you're the best vet I've ever come across, and you've a mind sharper than one of your scalpels, but you have much to learn about conservation. The key is always to get the local people on your side. Long after we've gone, the villagers will still be here. They are the true guardians of the land. We're just visitors.'

That made Frazer smile. Usually it was *him* receiving the lecture from his dad.

'Anyway,' said Bluey, joining in, 'we might need the help of these guys in finding the snake. It could be anywhere by now, and if it's just the three of us then it could take forever to track it down.'

Hal spoke again to the headman and to Anand. Other villagers joined in, each pointing in a different direction.

Finally a young boy grabbed Frazer's arm and dragged him to an area on the edge of the clearing, saying, 'Come! Come!'

'Dad . . . guys,' said Frazer, raising his voice above the hubbub, 'I think you should see this.'

The others came over and Frazer showed them the flattened area of vegetation leading away into the jungle.

'Looks like you found the trail, son,' said Hal.

'It was my friend here,' said Frazer, and was repaid with a big smile from the boy.

Hal spoke briefly to the headman, and a dozen young men – and one sharp-eyed small boy – were allocated to join them in the hunt.

The Trackers had the latest in snake-capturing equipment – although it still looked rather primitive to Frazer. Bluey carried a snake hook – an aluminium rod about two metres long with a strong steel hook at the end. Frazer knew that this was more a tool for handling smaller poisonous snakes, but it would still come in useful if they had to fend the animal off. Hal carried the snare pole – another long metal rod, hollow this time, and with a wire noose at the business end. The wire that formed the noose was fed through the middle of the hollow rod and emerged at the handle. Pulling the wire tightened the noose – hopefully round the snake's head.

Miranda had her medical kit containing the single most important piece of equipment – a syringe with a drug to safely sedate the snake, once it had been caught with the hook and snare.

Finally one of the villagers was given a large hessian sack to carry the snake in.

'We're gonna need a bigger bag,' said Frazer. But nobody heard him as they set off into the jungle.

The going was tough. The villagers went ahead of them, cutting a path through the vegetation with machetes, but that didn't help with the tangle of roots and stems, interspersed with slippery mud at their feet. It was still light, but Frazer knew that in the tropics the night falls fast.

The young village boy who'd shown him the trail was sticking by his side.

'What's your name, kid?'

'My name Randeep.'

'Well, Randeep, I'm kinda hoping we catch this

snake before it's dark. One of my least favourite activities is looking for things that might eat me in the dark. Not to mention the bugs . . .'

The boy just smiled.

As the trek continued, and afternoon began to fade into evening, so the mosquitoes came into their element.

'THIS is why I hate the jungle,' said Frazer, slapping at another mozzie whining in his ear. 'Seriously,' he said, loudly enough for the other Trackers ahead of him to hear, 'next time I want to go to the Antarctic or some place without bugs.'

'You want snakes, then you get bugs,' said Bluey. 'It's one of the laws of the jungle.'

'I can live without snakes,' said Frazer. 'Much prefer dolphins. No bugs in the sea.'

'I seem to remember that you and Zonnie had a little difficulty with a certain hungry squid, not that long ago . . .' Bluey smiled.

'But at least you can see the squid before it eats you,' replied Frazer, having another futile swipe at his tormentors.

Every few metres the party halted, as Hal stooped to examine a broken grass stem or flattened fern or a groove in the wet earth. Each time he emitted a satisfied little grunt. *Yes*, Frazer thought. *It means we're still on the monster's trail.*

After an hour of the trek, all conversation had stopped. Frazer found himself at the back of the straggling line, with just the ever-faithful Randeep for company. He felt weighed down by the heat and the bugs and the drudgery. He was wishing that Amazon were there to keep him on his toes.

Frazer had never had that many friends of his own age – he'd moved around between schools, and even been home-tutored by Hal, so he'd never quite found a gang of kids to hang out with. The Trackers – especially Bluey – had filled the void.

But with Zonnie it was something different. Maybe it was the whole cousins thing, or maybe it was their shared love of animals and adventure, but they'd just clicked from the start. True, they argued plenty, but each one knew that the other had their back, and would always be there for them.

Then Frazer was jerked out of his thoughts. There was some sort of commotion ahead. By now – under the enclosing canopy of the trees – it was dark, and the only light came from the torches held by the people at the head of the line. The daytime jungle noises – the screeching of the birds, the agitated chattering of the monkeys – had gone, replaced by the dry night noises of insects and the wetter burping of invisible frogs.

Frazer was pretty sure what was happening. They had found the snake and were going to capture it. Well, he'd come all this way and he was definitely not going to miss out on the exciting part. It'd be like eating your broccoli and skipping dessert.

He began to hurry forward to join in the fun, but then something stopped him in his tracks. There was a racket up in the trees, behind him and to the right. He pulled out his own powerful little torch and aimed the beam up into the branches. There he saw the unmistakable shapes of monkeys. For a brief moment he thought it was the macaques, and that he might be able to somehow retrieve his phone. But then he spotted the long tails and realized that they were langurs.

No real surprise, of course, seeing a monkey in a tree in India, but it was unusual to see them so active at this time of day. They had normally settled down by dusk, high in the canopy, where they would be safe from leopards and other predators. But these langurs had definitely not settled down. They were highly agitated.

And Frazer had an idea why.

He yelled, 'Hey, Dad, Bluey, Miranda . . .' but the others had already moved on far ahead. He thought quickly and then said to Randeep, 'Hurry, tell my father that I think I've found the snake. They must come back quickly.'

And then he plunged after the monkeys into the deep jungle.

9

An Indian Banquet

'Answer, please just answer,' said Amazon, as she listened to the electronic ringing of the phone. After seven rings, the phone went to voicemail. Amazon resisted the urge to curse.

'It's Miranda – she's the traitor in TRACKS . . .'

She began telling the story in a rapid, staccato voice, but halfway through a sentence a recorded voice said, 'Voicemail full,' and she was cut off.

'Clear your messages, Frazer, you imbecile!' she yelled. But then she realized that all she had to do was to get the story to Drexler. He would know what to do.

Amazon got dressed as smartly as she could manage – the last thing she wanted was to stand out. She found one of her school skirts at the bottom of her case and a pair of unladdered tights, and a blouse that she had no recollection of ever having bought or worn. She washed the furious tears from her face, brushed her hair, cleaned her teeth and, finally, shone her shoes with her dirty T-shirt. She checked herself in the mirror.

She'd never looked quite this uncool.

It didn't matter. Getting to Drexler was all that counted. She opened the door to her room and found the servant there, blocking the doorway.

'I need to get to Doctor Drexler,' she said imploringly. 'It's a matter of life and death!'

The servant just stared at her, and when she tried to push past him he put his hand on her arm and forced her – gently – back. Then he pointed at the ornate clock on the wall and grunted.

'I know it's not time, but I need to see . . . oh, what's the use.'

And then she twisted away and made a dart for the door. But the servant was too quick and caught her before she could escape. He pushed her back inside and locked the door. She beat against the heavy wood until her knuckles were raw, to no avail.

There must be another way out. She looked over her balcony, but there was no way down, not even a drainpipe to cling on to. So she would have to wait the twenty minutes till the banquet before she could tell Drexler what she knew. And what a story it was.

The message of the diary was clear. The dying embers of the fire under which it was hidden had done much damage, but the fake burn and ageing effects had been put there to disguise the still legible truth that she had read in her father's writing.

Ling-Mei saw it first. We'd found out from Sergei that the animals were being smuggled out and sent to some sort of secret reserve. Except it's not a reserve. We don't yet know exactly what its purpose is, but we do know it is not to preserve anything except the profits of the investors.

I didn't want to believe the evidence, but Ling-Mei doesn't have my . . . history. She pointed out that only one organization had links here in central Asia, in Siberia, in Africa and in Oceania. And then there was the evidence of the paperwork, the documents. Not all the animals had been smuggled out illegally. Some of them seemed to have the correct permits. And those permits had been authorized by someone at TRACKS.

There are only two alternatives. Either TRACKS is an evil organization, with my brother the monster-in-chief or there's a traitor deep in the heart of the organization, betraying it and my brother and everything they stand for.

A few pages later came another revelation.

It's Kaggs. I know it now. Somehow he's in league with the traitor at TRACKS. Together they are spiriting animals away from their natural environment, and taking them . . . where?

There was that name Kaggs again. Amazon drummed her fingers impatiently on the laptop. Uncle Hal had told her he was evil, that he had tried to kill the Hunt brothers many times. And now he was working together with the TRACKS traitor. The traitor that Amazon knew was Miranda Coverdale.

Although it had been a shock at first, on reflection it seemed so obvious. She was never particularly friendly, never open, never revealed anything of herself. Amazon didn't even know where she was from.

Well, that didn't matter now. Amazon knew where she and this villain Kaggs were going: straight to jail.

At that moment there was a knock at the door. She went to it and the silent servant beckoned her. He touched her hand as she passed, giving it a gentle squeeze. Amazon was astonished by the gesture, but somehow it comforted her – made her feel a little less alone. She tried to smile at him, but his back was to her as he led her down the corridor.

As they walked, other guests appeared in the hallway, emerging from rooms into which she glanced, and saw were even grander and more ornate than her own. There were Indian ladies draped in golden jewellery, their fine saris glittering in the candlelight – for yes, the palace was lit both with electric chandeliers and by thousands of candles that had appeared since Amazon had arrived. The ladies were escorted by tall Indian men, some in military uniform, others in traditional dress, with white turbans and the long, intricately embroidered coats called sherwanis.

There were also Europeans and Americans, some smartly dressed, others more casual. Most of them seemed to be men. Amazon followed her guide down the huge staircase – even more imposing now that the space below it was busy with people and dancing with the golden light of the candles.

But Amazon was determined not to be distracted. She had to tell Drexler about the traitor. She strained to look for him through the crowd. But she had never felt so small, and all she could see once she reached the bottom of the stairs was the backs of the adults, as they all formed a pulsing, glittering stream, headed towards the dining room.

They entered another huge room, Amazon bobbing and weaving, trying to get to Drexler. This room was as long as a cathedral aisle, with a roof beautifully painted, showing elephants and tigers battling together, and more processions of beautiful maidens and handsome princes. A table, almost as long as the room, was set with heavy silver cutlery, crystal wine glasses and white plates with golden rims.

Despite her agitation and frustration, Amazon

sensed that this was quite the most beautiful dining arrangement she had ever seen, although in truth that wasn't saying much. The dining room at her boarding school was grey and tatty and grubby, and everything smelled of cabbage.

She suddenly found that she was being guided into a seat – she wasn't quite sure how, just that there was a subtle pressure on her, both pulling and pushing. She was sitting almost at the head of the great table, with a tall elderly lady on one side and a small kindly-looking man on the other. He was wearing a tweed jacket and an old shirt, a little frayed at the collar. With his reading glasses on a chain around his neck, he looked like an absent-minded professor.

'How nice to have young people at the table,' said the tall lady, in a voice loud enough to stop a charging rhino. And her tone managed to convey the message that in fact it was not at all nice to have young people at the table or anywhere else for that matter. 'I expect,' she continued, 'that you're one of the Maharaja's little projects.'

Amazon was about to reply that she was nobody's little project, but the lady was already talking across her at the sweet little man.

Amazon looked round the table and finally saw Drexler. He was right at the far end. He appeared to be deep in conversation with a senior army officer on one side and a tall African gentleman on the other. But she got the distinct impression that he was secretly keeping a close eye on her. She mouthed, 'I NEED TO TALK,' at him and began to stand up, but he made a calming motion with his hands. At the same time she heard a gentle voice from her side.

'I do so hate these formal events. If it were up to me, I would only ever eat my supper on a tray in front of the TV.'

Amazon was sure that the man had been speaking to her, but the tall lady replied, 'Oh, I quite agree, Maharaja. I myself am a great fan of *Ready Steady Cook* and *X Factor*. I . . .'

'Lady Stanmoor,' said the little man, 'would you mind terribly if I talked for a short while with my friend here? We have many things to discuss.'

And Amazon realized that she was sitting next to the owner of the palace.

'I am very, very pleased to meet you, Amazon,' he said. 'I knew your father and your grandfather well. We often spent time together collecting animals back when I was only a little older than you.'

'You knew my dad . . .?' said Amazon. Ever since her parents had disappeared, she cherished any scraps of information about them, the way that a starving child might nurse a crust of bread.

'Oh, indeed. In a reversal of expectation, the American taught the Indian how to ride an elephant! He was something of a natural at the art.'

'I didn't think maharajas rode their own elephants,' replied a smiling Amazon. 'Don't you have a mahout to do that for you, while you sit on that nice comfy cabin on the back . . .?'

'The howdah. Indeed, you are right, young lady. And I believe it somewhat scandalized the servants. Is that not so, Mehmet?'

The Maharaja was looking at the space behind Amazon. She turned and saw that the silent servant was there, standing to attention. He seemed flustered by the Maharaja's direct address and merely bowed.

'So he knew my father too?' Amazon said excitedly. 'I'd love to speak to him . . . Oh, but he can't seem to speak English . . .'

'No, he cannot,' said the Maharaja sadly. 'I'm afraid he has literally lost his tongue. An accident, long ago.'

'How terrible!' gasped Amazon. She desperately wanted to know what sort of accident, but stopped herself from asking. It seemed such bad manners . . .

Over the next fifteen minutes the Maharaja asked her many questions about her school and other aspects of life in England, and then about her work with TRACKS. He seemed very well informed about their activities. He already knew all about the family of Amur leopards they had rescued in the far east of Russia, and about the baby leatherback turtles they had saved in Polynesia. He even knew about their most recent adventure in the Canadian wilderness. He asked her about the animals they had encountered, and she told him about the bears and mountain lions and wolves. The Maharaja's eyes lit up, and he said, 'Ah, what fine additions they would make to any collection . . . .'

As they spoke, the food arrived. Amazon had supposed that they would be served European cuisine at such a grand occasion, but all the dishes were Indian, with grilled meats and wonderful hot curries coming thick and fast, all cooked with such delicacy and precision that Amazon could taste each complex flavour separately, even as they blended together to form a harmonious whole. Even the rice tasted good – not bland and stodgy like she was used to back at school, but light and fluffy and bursting with taste. She hadn't realized that something so simple could be so delicious.

The wonderful food didn't make her forget that she had to go and tell Drexler about her discovery, but, each time she tried to move, the Maharaja would ask her another question, pinning her to her seat. She was just too polite and well brought up to walk away while he was talking to her.

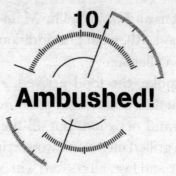

10

Ambushed!

At that moment, banquets were the very last thing on Frazer Hunt's mind.

What *was* at the forefront of his mind was how deeply unpleasant it might feel to be killed by a giant reticulated python in the humid murk of the jungle.

He knew that he had been stupid. He had wandered along under the trees, looking upwards, trying to get a precise fix on where the snake was from the behaviour of the langurs. And he was ninety-nine per cent sure that it was the snake that had got the monkeys worked up into such a lather. Snakes were ambush predators, which meant that they were essentially harmless as long as the prey knew that they were there, and could keep them in sight. The langurs had obviously spotted the snake and were letting the whole jungle know about it.

Frazer did have one small worm of doubt wriggling in the back of his mind. Ninety-nine per cent is not quite the same as one hundred per cent. That one per cent floating around could just be the one per cent that killed him.

His dad had always told him that safety first was the principle he should apply to everything – and that meant meticulous preparation and rational risk minimization. It didn't matter that, when Hal was a boy, he had done a thousand reckless and lunatic things himself – that's if even half the stories told by and about him were true. But he had drilled the idea into Frazer that he should at least be aware of possible dangers, and so Frazer knew that there was always the chance that the langurs hadn't spotted the snake, but some other hunter. A leopard or even a tiger. If that were the case, then he would be in serious trouble.

But no, surely there wouldn't be more than one top predator in this one little patch of jungle . . .

Suddenly he felt a pain of such intensity that all the complicated clutter of thoughts and images and half-formed ideas and future hopes and dreams that jostled in his head was instantly obliterated, to be replaced by a single, intense white light.

11

The Snake in the Grass

At last she had her chance. A man with a spotted bow tie, and a moustache like a hairy snail crawling across his face, had finally managed to get the host's attention, and was now talking at him about the Maharaja's famous collection of vintage cars. At that moment she saw Drexler wipe his mouth on a napkin, excuse himself and leave the table.

Amazon darted quickly after him before he could reach the bathroom or wherever he was headed. She caught up with him in one of the many corridors snaking away from the dining room like the tentacles of an octopus.

'Doctor,' she panted, 'I have to tell you –'

Drexler, clearly sensing the urgency and importance of whatever it was that Amazon wanted to say, looked nervously around, and silenced her with a raised hand.

'Not here,' he whispered. 'It's not safe. Follow me.'

He opened a door leading off from the corridor

and they entered a room. It was a library, the shelves going all the way from floor to ceiling. Heavy leather chairs were scattered around.

Drexler sat in one chair and told Amazon to sit down opposite him. 'What is this, Amazon?' he asked, in his usual unemotional way. 'And do please be concise – we mustn't be away from the banquet for too long . . .'

And then, in a gush, Amazon told him what she knew.

'There's a traitor in TRACKS. Someone is helping this Kaggs character to steal animals and smuggle them to some place where . . . I don't know, where something terrible happens to them. It's all in my father's diary. When Uncle Hal rescued it from the fire, it looked pretty bad. But whoever digitized it managed to rescue most of the text. But then they covered it all up again, in fact, made it worse. And they left their digital signature on it. It was Miranda – Miranda Coverdale. We've got to tell Uncle Hal. She's with them now, looking for that snake. Who knows what she's going to do . . .'

Drexler was not one to show his emotions. At the mention of Miranda Coverdale his eyes opened a little more widely behind his rimless spectacles.

'You say you have proof of all this?'

'Yes, on my laptop. I . . .'

Then Amazon stopped herself. She just couldn't admit that she'd copied the document from Drexler's laptop. 'I, er, emailed it to my laptop from my iPad. And then I was able to analyse it properly.'

'I see.'

Drexler said nothing for what seemed like ages to Amazon then he sprang to his feet with surprising energy.

'Wait here. I will go and get a message sent to Mr Hunt. It may take a little while to get through, but that can't be helped.'

He swept from the room, leaving Amazon feeling a little bewildered. She stood up and went over to the stacks of books. Most were ancient leather-backed editions. Multi-volume works of history and geography. There were also many beautiful books about animals. One giant book of bird paintings came up to Amazon's waist. She heaved it up on to a desk and looked through it. The paintings were all life-sized.

Amazon's hands were in her pockets as she gazed at a wonderfully vibrant and dramatic picture of a bald eagle – it reminded her of those she had seen in Canada, not very long ago. Then her fingers brushed against a scrap of paper. She pulled it out and unfolded it. The writing was neat and careful, but also curiously awkward, as if written by someone whose first language was not English.

Little Lady,

Dr Drexler is very bad man. You must run away. I was friend of your father many years ago. He saved my life from tiger. I owe him this. I cannot help more. All here is bad. Run, run fast away.

Friend of her father . . . Could it have been the mute servant, what was his name . . .? Mehmet? Amazon thought perhaps that she remembered him brushing against her . . .

She stared at the note, not quite believing what it was saying. And then, without consciously understanding the reasons why, she knew she had to do as the note ordered and run. She reached the door just as it was opening.

In front of her she saw the kindly face of the Maharaja. Now he was standing up, she could see just how tiny he was – the same height as her.

'Oh, sir,' she gushed. 'I need your help. My father . . . he's in danger. Doctor Drexler is . . .'

'My dear girl,' said the Maharaja, 'I know quite well what Doctor Drexler is.'

And then Amazon saw that, in the darkness behind him, other figures loomed. The Maharaja came forward into the library. Two more of his men were with him – they looked like the mounted guards Amazon had seen at the gates – as tall and intimidating as the Maharaja was short and gentle. And behind them, in turn, came Dr Drexler, his face frozen and emotionless.

'But . . . but . . .' was all that Amazon could say.

'I truly am sorry, my dear child,' said the Maharaja with a little giggle. 'We had hoped that there would be no need to involve you in all this unpleasantness.

I have no desire, truly, to harm innocents. But you have forced our hand.'

'You,' said Amazon, looking at Drexler. 'You're the traitor, aren't you?'

Her voice was filled with bitterness, loathing, despair.

'Traitor? No, not traitor,' said Drexler, his voice now drier, colder, deader than ever.

'But you've betrayed my Uncle Hal and everything TRACKS stands for. And for what? Money?'

'Money? No, never money.'

'Then why?'

'We have a little time, so I will tell you a story,' said Drexler, calmly returning to the leather chair he had previously occupied. 'I helped to set up TRACKS with your father and your uncle. They, of course, took all the credit, garnered all the glory. It was *their* profiles that appeared in the colour supplements of the Sunday newspapers. I was always working in the background. But I did not mind, did not complain, because of my dedication to science. All along I had a great scheme, a plan, an opportunity to make TRACKS the most illustrious scientific organization in the world. I had laid down the theoretical foundation for a breakthrough of earth-shattering impact.

'I took my theory and my findings, along with a fully costed proposal to undertake the enterprise, to Hal Hunt. He could see that what I envisaged made scientific sense. He knew that I could accomplish this great feat, that I could harness the resources of TRACKS to change the world. But he said no! No! He said no to the greatest achievement in the history of science!'

Drexler had become, by his standards, very animated, his voice getting louder until he was almost shouting. But then he recovered his composure and continued in his dry, level tone. 'And that is why I had to look elsewhere for help with this. And it was natural that I should go to my great benefactor.'

Drexler bowed towards the Maharaja, and the little man smiled and nodded back.

'He had some of the resources necessary. But, although rich in land, he was . . .'

Here the Maharaja took over.

'Yes, yes, ever since the end of the good old days when the British ruled India through we great landowners, the Indian state has stolen and swindled us out of our wealth. And so, understanding as I did the great project that my good friend Doctor Drexler was attempting, I had to bring in a . . . business partner, let us say.

'This man Kaggs, whom you mentioned to Doctor Drexler. He is not a . . . *nice* man. But he knows about money. And so on my reserve in the south, a unique and special place, we set up both a scientific research station and a . . . well, my dear, you shall find out what it is we have set up there.'

'Why? What do you mean?'

'It is time, I think,' said Drexler, 'for a family reunion.'

The Maharaja said something to the guards in Hindi. They began to move towards Amazon.

'What is this? What are . . .? I . . .' Then Amazon decided that it was time to do something she had never done before in her life. The scream for help, however, lasted less than a second. It was terminated by a hard hand, clamped round her mouth.

And then Amazon saw Dr Drexler open his medical case. She could not see what was inside until he raised his hands. In them was a gleaming metal and glass object, which it took her a moment to realize was the biggest syringe she had ever seen.

'I would like very much to be able to say that this will not hurt,' said the doctor, his voice suddenly softer. 'But I'm afraid that it will. But not for long, I promise you.'

And then one of the guards pulled up the sleeve of Amazon's school blouse and Drexler plunged in the needle.

He was right. It did hurt. But, even before Drexler had pulled it out again, the library around her dimmed and darkened, and then Amazon Hunt was dead to the world.

12

Squeezed!

Such was the shock, Frazer didn't know straight away that he had been bitten. For a second, he thought that he had blundered into a thorn bush.

But his mind had, at a deeper level, registered the blur of the long shape and the snap of the broad head, and he certainly felt the searing pain in his upper arm and the brute strength that had hurled him back on to the floor of the jungle.

And then the fear and the pain and the panic tumbled and surged together in his head. He yelped and flapped and kicked, half expecting to find the snake's deadly coils already encircling him.

But there was nothing. Nothing, that is, except for the shock and pain of the bite. And then he thought he saw the sinuous form of the snake retreat back into the deeper murk of the undergrowth, and the darkness made it seem even more monstrous.

But the fact that the snake had released him meant, Frazer realized, that it had probably been a defensive strike, intended to warn him off. *Back off!* it said. *Back off!*

He peered into the darkness around him, his every sense alive. There was not a sound from the jungle. The langurs had fled through the treetops, leaving him to his fate. He put his fingers to his arm. The teeth had punctured his jacket and penetrated the flesh, like a fork going through mashed potato. But, despite the pain, the wound did not, in reality, seem too bad. Blood, at least, wasn't gushing through the holes in his jacket. He guessed that the needle-like teeth had merely punctured the muscle, but not torn through it or raked it away from the bone.

'Nice snaky snaky,' he said softly, as he slowly raised himself from the leafy ground. He hoped that Randeep had found his father, and that help was coming.

He began to edge away. As he did so, he eased his rucksack off his back. It contained one of his most prized possessions – a machete he had been given by a Polynesian friend, on an island in the South Pacific. Frazer would never hurt an animal if there were any alternative, but he'd decided that when confronting a giant snake you really do want a long, sharp weapon in your hand.

He'd have felt much more comfortable if he'd known where the snake was. He stared into the blackness around him, convinced that every root and vine was a giant serpent, tasting the air with its thin tongue.

But there was nothing to see, and he breathed a little more easily. His hand was still fishing inside his rucksack for the machete, which was caught up in something.

Time, he decided, to yell for help.

He got as far as taking a deep breath when the snake struck again, coming at him from right under his feet. The whole time he had been backing towards it, rather than away. This was going to be the death grip – the bite it used to hold its prey still long enough to loop the killing coils round its body.

A cavernous jaw surged up towards him, two rows of razor-sharp white daggers, glinting in the fading light. Frazer instinctively threw up his arm in defence – the arm that was still thrust inside the backpack.

A juddering surge of pain swept through his forearm and there was a muffled crunch as teeth pierced the contents of his bag and clamped down on fabric, machete and flesh.

The bag and its contents gave him some protection, but still he was caught like a rat in a trap. gripping could feel the gripping teeth, and knew that if he tried to pull his arm free he would rake his flesh from the bone. So he put all his might into three hard punches to the snake's head, delivered with his left fist – the one outside the bag.

They were good punches, but it was like punching rock – there was no give. And now the snake was able to engulf him in its coils, as quickly as water poured from a tap covers the ice in a glass.

'Aaaarrgghh!' Frazer managed a scream or rather a short guttural shout of rage and frustration. He did not plan to die like this, the life squeezed out of him by some big dumb reptile.

It was another mistake. To scream meant to exhale and, as he exhaled, the python squeezed again. That was the killer's technique – to squeeze each time its prey breathed out. Death would come in a very few minutes.

Frazer tried to remember everything he had been taught about snakes. The problem was that almost all of it was about handling poisonous snakes, not giant constrictors. A spitting cobra or a deadly poisonous krait he could have fought, but the thing that held him now seemed utterly invulnerable.

Frazer was getting light-headed. The pain from the bites was less, and even the terrible ache from the squeezing round his middle seemed to have diminished a little, but he knew that that was because he was beginning to fade away, to lose consciousness.

And that meant death. And, after death, the thing that was even worse than death: being swallowed, whole, and slowly digested over a couple of weeks by the strong acids in the snake's gut.

Something.

He had to do something.

He tried to withdraw the arm holding his machete inside the rucksack, but it was impossible: the teeth held him like a vice. A vice as sharp as broken glass.

And then Frazer remembered something about alcohol . . .

He'd read that if you were ever grabbed by a python you could pour a little alcohol on its head and it would let go. He had some hand sanitizer in his rucksack, and hand sanitizer contains alcohol, but there was just no way to reach it.

And then, from somewhere deep in his subconscious, another memory floated up. The tail. The python's tail. Strange to think of a snake as having a tail – it seemed, in a way, *all* tail. But the last section of that long body – the area behind the tiny bones that were all that remained of its long-lost back legs – was the tail, and it was, he recalled, highly sensitive.

Frazer still had one hand free. The snake was colossal, but most of it was wrapped round his body. He followed the coils with his eye and saw, there on the jungle floor, the twitching tail. It was as thick as his arm, but tapered to a point. He stretched for it with his left arm, and felt the python's jaws tense and tighten round the rucksack that enclosed his other arm, the needle-pointed teeth digging in just a little deeper.

He was so close to the snake's head now that he could see the starlight glinting in its yellow eyes. There was no malice or evil there, Frazer saw, just the relentless, implacable hunger that drove it to kill without thought or mercy.

The tail wriggled a couple of centimetres out of reach. Frazer knew that this was his last chance to avoid death. He made one last huge effort, lunging against the weight of the beast that surrounded him, and YES! His fingers caught and then gripped the tail. He had only a second to do what he had to do – as soon as the snake realized what was happening, it would simply send a shimmer through its great length and shake its tail free.

And so, using his last reserve of energy, Frazer yanked the scaly tail towards his mouth and bit down, crunching through the scales and flesh until he reached the bone below.

The effect was instantaneous. The python hissed like water poured on a raging fire, flinched, writhed, uncoiled and lurched away. Frazer dragged some air into his lungs. There was a sharp pain in his chest. Not quite enough to signal a cracked rib, but it still hurt like hell. But there was no time to worry about that now or about the two bites – one nasty, one superficial. The snake would be back and now it was mad as well as hungry.

Frazer pulled the machete out of the rucksack. The blade was slick with blood that had run down from his bitten arm. He reached in again to get the hand sanitizer. His plan was to squirt it in the mouth and eyes of the python as it lunged. Then he'd go in with the machete.

It was black night now. He recovered the torch from his pocket. The snake could smell and taste him in the air, and he needed to even things up by giving himself the chance to see it.

He pressed the 'on' button and stuck the torch in his mouth. The strong beam lit up a circle of jungle that moved as he turned his head. He panicked when he couldn't see the snake, and spun wildly, convinced it was behind him.

But then he found it again, right in front of him. It was moving slowly towards him, its eyes fixed on him, its tongue tasting the air.

For the first time Frazer was able to get a good look at the beast. Its colours were muted by the torchlight, and the creature looked a muddy grey. But the size was truly awesome. Frazer could not believe that he had managed to escape from such a monster.

This is gonna be one heck of a story, he thought. *If I survive . . .*

And then he realized that he should be screaming for help. The trouble was that his mouth was full of torch. He backed away and tried to shout with the torch in his mouth, but all that came out was a muffled, *'Nnnnnngthhhh.'*

And then the torch fell out of his mouth. He tried to catch it and dropped his machete. At the same moment the python struck, firing itself at him like a harpoon the size of a tree. Frazer staggered back and squirted the hand-sanitizer gel at the python's face. As he did, he sensed movement all around him.

It's Dad, he thought. *He's here to save me.*

The snake's strike never hit home. A big canvas tarpaulin was hurled over it.

Strange, thought Frazer, *I don't remember us having anything like that with us . . .*

A dozen bodies leapt on top of the covered snake, wrestling to control it.

There was a snap as a foot stepped on a twig behind him and Frazer turned, expecting to see the face of his father, and maybe Bluey as well, grinning that huge grin of his.

But it was not his father or his friend.

It was another face that he'd come to know rather well, back in the South Seas.

A look of horror crossed Frazer's face. The snake may have been contained, but he was still in grave danger.

He tried to shout, but this time he was stopped, not by the encircling coils of the world's biggest snake, but by a rough cloth clamped over his mouth. His nose filled with a sweet chemical smell. He tried not to breathe, but it was impossible. The last thing he saw before he lost consciousness was the leering face of Leopold Chung, animal collector, gangster and, quite possibly, lunatic, looming over him.

Part 2: Hunted

13

Amazon's Journey

Amazon didn't want to get up. It was cold outside. Heck, it was cold inside! The headmistress was so mean she never let them put the central heating on unless the duck pond in the grounds was frozen solid. Her bed was the only warm spot in the entire universe and she wasn't getting out of it. Certainly there was nothing on the breakfast menu that could tempt her. In fact, could you even call it a menu when it contained only one item: porridge? It wasn't even good porridge. It was made from old tweed jackets and earwax. If you were a goody two-shoes or a prefect, you got a dollop of jam in your porridge. But Amazon wasn't a goody two-shoes. She was always getting into trouble.

So, no, she would stay right here in bed and keep warm.

Anyway, outside the bed it wasn't just cold. There was something else there. Something . . . *not nice*.

The trouble was that her bed kept moving. It was

rocking from side to side, as if she were on a ship. That must be it: she was on a ship. And that's why she felt seasick.

But no, that still wasn't it. There was something she had to do. Her homework? She imagined a sheet of impossible equations she was supposed to solve. She stared at the numbers and indecipherable squiggles. There was a meaning in the numbers, in the shapes. She stared more closely, pulling the paper close to her eye. Close enough for her to see that the shapes were not abstract, but tiny pictures. She peered again, touching her eyeball with the paper. At last she could see what it all was.

It was the sinuous form of a snake. And it was growing ever larger by the second. It soon filled the page. It was a monstrous hybrid of a python and a cobra – it could poison or crush you as it chose. And now it was bigger than the page, bigger than her bed, bigger than her room. She screamed, but no noise came out of her mouth. The snake drew back and, with a vicious crack that resounded through her world, slapped her.

Amazon was suddenly wide awake, but some instinct told her to keep her eyes shut. Her face stung, and her head felt as though there were a giant snake trying to get out of it, using her eyeball as the main exit.

She was on the floor of some kind of vehicle. A truck probably. A truck that was bouncing over a rough road. Her mind was still foggy, half trapped in the drugged dream she'd been having. And yes, she knew she'd been drugged – that syringe.

'Girl not wake up,' said a voice. It belonged to the man who had just hit her. She sensed that he was looming over her, and she could smell the garlic on his breath. He sounded eastern European, perhaps Russian. Amazon fought the urge to scream and struggle. If they thought she was still unconscious, she might learn something vital. 'Still in drug. Sleep like baby.'

'We do not need to hit,' came another voice. Amazon thought that it belonged to an Indian. 'The boss says we have got to keep her safe.'

The first man grunted, and Amazon felt him moving away. 'I don't like screamers,' he grouched.

Amazon tried to get her brain working.

Drexler.

The diary.

The Maharaja.

She tried to make them fit together so she could understand what was going on. Her thoughts were interrupted by the voices.

'How far to hunting place?'

'An hour, maybe two.'

Hunting place? What could that mean?

Well, she didn't plan on finding out. Very carefully Amazon opened her eyelids to admit a sliver of light. She saw that she'd been half right about the truck.

She was in the back of an old four-wheel-drive vehicle. She was lying on the floor. On one side of her she saw the Russian – he was wearing a sharp dark suit, which seemed wrong both for his voice and for India – that's if they were still in India . . .

The other person was a slender Indian, with spectacles and a thin moustache. He looked like a harmless small-town pharmacist.

Beyond them were the back doors of the jeep. They were the sort that swung open to the sides. Amazon was too low down to see out of the windows, or rather all she could see was what may have been blue sky, at times interrupted by green leaves as they passed under and between trees. She knew that there was no point trying to escape if they were in the middle of nowhere. Even if she managed to leap out of the vehicle, they'd just run after her and bring her back.

What she needed was people. She'd come to know and love the ordinary Indians, who seemed always so kind and so gentle. If she threw herself on their mercy, they'd help her, she knew they would.

She just needed the right moment to act.

Eventually, after a nerve-wracking half-hour, it came.

The driver cursed, and at the same moment Amazon heard the lowing of water buffalo and the excited chatter of a group of people. She hoped against hope that they were driving through a village or settlement. She imagined a crossroads with villagers milling around, and the street full of men and women and children and dogs, as well as the buffalo and bony cattle you saw everywhere in rural India.

It was now or never.

She sprang for the door, passing right between the startled guards. The Indian was slow, but the Russian moved with surprising speed. He half grabbed her, but she twisted out of his grip and made it to the door. There was a handle – again she had to hope that it was unlocked.

She was in luck! She turned it, pushed and suddenly she was out in the hot, dry air. For a second she was dazzled by the light, as well as baked by the heat. She was right about the water buffalo – they were all around. Beautiful blue-grey beasts, huge but placid.

And there were people. A couple of old men with loose turbans, carrying long sticks that they used to nudge and guide the buffalo in the right direction. And some children. A woman with an earthenware jar on her head. But there was no village, no crossroad, no crowd.

'Help . . . please help me,' she said, her voice cracking with fear and emotion and the dryness of her mouth. 'These men . . . they've kidnapped me. They want to hurt me. Please . . .'

The figures stared back at her, uncomprehending. And a little fearful.

Suddenly she was grabbed from behind, a hand on each of her shoulders. There was no way she could run.

It was the Russian who had her. The Indian spoke a few words to the peasants, who listened in silence, their faces still showing no emotion. Amazon looked around her as the man spoke, trying to gauge where she was. The land was much greener than the places she had visited up until now, in the north of the country. They were in an area of fairly open forest, with tall trees leaning gracefully over them.

But it was not the natural features that made her gasp. Further along the road they were travelling on she could see a huge wall that stretched, it seemed, for miles on either side. It looked ancient, as if created by some long-dead civilization.

But she had no more time to gape. The Russian seized her by the hair and forced her back into the truck.

'Blindfold her,' said the Indian. Dutifully, the Russian tore a strip from a piece of filthy cloth, before placing the rag over Amazon's eyes. She winced in pain as he tugged fiercely on the cloth, binding it in a tight knot.

'That was a silly thing to do,' the Indian continued. 'There is nowhere for you to run to. And all of the peasants in this area belong to their feudal lord.'

'The Maharaja of Jaipod,' said Amazon bitterly.

'That is correct.'

'What are you going to do with me?'

'All will soon be revealed.'

'Hands?' said the Russian.

'Oh yes, hands,' said the Indian, and the Russian tied them tightly behind her back.

It was incredibly uncomfortable, but luckily it didn't last long.

The truck drove on for another half an hour. Amazon guessed they must have passed through a gateway in the wall and were now . . . where? In whatever lay beyond it.

They pulled up and the Russian dragged her out. Unable to see, she felt utterly helpless. She stumbled on some steps and then sensed that they had moved indoors. Footsteps echoed on a hard marble floor. Then the echoes changed and Amazon thought she had moved into a bigger space. She heard a hubbub, as if a group of people were talking excitedly.

The blindfold was removed from her eyes. She was in a large room, hung with beautiful tapestries that shimmered with deep reds and lines of gold thread. There were men standing around. A few she thought she recognized from the banquet the day before. Others were new to her. Some were sleek-looking, with hard faces and cold eyes. Others were overweight and doughy, their tiny eyes squeezed between folds of fat, bald heads glistening in the electric light.

The tall African she'd seen at the banquet was there as well, his face stern and unyielding.

The men looked at her and laughed or murmured to each other. She found their gazes unbearable. She saw the Maharaja, a glass in his hand, his voice as friendly and bubbly as the champagne he was drinking. The Russian gave her a sharp shove and she stumbled forward.

'You filthy, cowardly scumbag,' she spat, meaning it for the Russian, but it fitted the Maharaja as well.

Then the Maharaja turned and saw her. His face hardened.

'Not here, you fools!' he said. 'Take her down with the others.'

He waved his hand and she was dragged out of the room by the Russian thug. She aimed a kick, but he evaded her easily, and cuffed the back of her head lightly, but in a way that said 'do that again and I'll hurt you'.

She managed to get a rough sense of the place as she was shoved and shunted. This wasn't a palace like the one she had been in the day before. It was large, but not *that* large.

The Russian kicked a wooden door open and pulled her down a narrow spiralling stone stairway. She stumbled twice, but he stopped her from falling on her face – she would not have been able to save herself as her hands were still bound.

Now Amazon found herself in a long space

beneath the main hall where the men had leered and jeered at her. There was a strong smell in the air. It was heavy – nauseating almost – and yet, to her, oddly comforting. It was the smell of animals. Yes, animals had been kept down here. Big ones. Small ones. Hunters. Hunted.

It took her eyes a couple of seconds to grow accustomed to the gloom, but she knew immediately that there was a cage and something was in it. The animals, she thought at first.

The cage was like something from backstage at the circus, or the kind of old-fashioned zoo where bored animals paced backwards and forwards, with despair or rage in their hearts.

It wasn't actually one long cage, as Amazon had first thought, but a series of smaller cages lined up next to each other. And each contained a living thing. An animal, yes, but a very special one.

A human being.

A person.

She moved forward until she touched the bars.

'Mum . . .' she said in a faltering voice, as her eyes filled with tears. 'Dad . . . Frazer . . .'

14

Frazer's Journey

Frazer's journey to the cage in the cellar of the hunting lodge of the Maharaja of Jaipod had been even less comfortable than that of his cousin, Amazon.

What made it particularly unpleasant were his travelling companions in the back of the big truck, although only one of them – the giant reticulated python – spent the entire journey with him.

It had begun with that suffocating cloth, saturated with chloroform. It had only put him under for a few minutes, but it was long enough for Chung and his gang of smugglers to get him and the snake away through the jungle. Frazer woke to find himself trussed up like a turkey, being carried over the shoulder of one of the thugs. The first thing he did was to puke up over the backs of the man's legs – one of the unfortunate side effects of chloroform. It was too gross to give Frazer any satisfaction, but that didn't stop the man from hurling him on the ground and kicking him in the ribs.

Chung came over and spoke sharply to the guy in Chinese. Then he said to Frazer, 'Good, you wake up. Now you run. You stop running and we have to shoot you, which would be a very great shame.'

To stop him from escaping, his guard slipped a length of rope round his neck. Frazer was very aware of the fact that, if he fell over, he'd get throttled. It greatly concentrated his mind.

There were about twenty of them – it took ten to carry the enormous body of the snake. They seemed to be heading on a circuit round the village and back to the road, jogging almost blind along narrow paths.

Frazer lost track of time – the fear and the pain and the nausea from the chloroform combined to make the jungle run more like a nightmare than a waking experience.

Twice he fell, but luckily each time there was just enough slack in the rope to save him from strangulation, and he was dragged back to his feet and urged on with harsh words.

Finally they reached the road and running became a little easier. Soon afterwards they found the truck and a cluster of jeeps. Frazer was bundled into the back of the truck with the snake and four of the men. The others climbed into the jeeps, and together the convoy rolled off into the night.

Frazer found himself tightly bound and lying on the bed of the truck next to the snake. It was still shrouded in thick canvas tarpaulin, and lay as still as death. It had obviously been tranquillized. But Frazer couldn't help but wonder what would happen when it eventually awoke.

'Don't worry, American kid, you're not food for the snake.'

It was Leopold Chung, riding, for the present, in the back with Frazer.

'What the heck are you doing here, Chung?' Frazer said, his voice a little shaky, both from the chloroform and the grim jungle trek. 'And how did you get off that island?'

Frazer and Amazon had last seen Leopold Chung as they paddled away on a home-made raft from a deserted island in Polynesia. Chung, working with a corrupt local chief, had been attempting to steal the baby turtles TRACKS were trying to protect. The same tropical storm that had swept the cousins to a tiny atoll also brought Chung there – half mad from drinking seawater and, Frazer suspected, his own urine. When the cousins had gone back with help to pick him up, there was no sign of the crafty animal smuggler.

Frazer found Chung both fascinating and repellent. He could appear completely insane one moment and then coldly rational the next. In fact, Frazer had come to the conclusion that most of his eccentricities were a sham, designed to make the world underestimate him.

'Like giant squid, Chung has many tentacles. They reach far. Also my men, they love their boss. They not let him die on island. Not like the murdering American boy and English girl.'

'Hey, it was *you* who tried to kill *us*! Anyway, we came back for you.'

Chung shrugged. 'Maybe, maybe not. But I guess, if you came back, it was to put Chung in jail. Well, Chung is not a man to be jailed.'

'We'll see about that,' said Frazer, with more confidence than he was actually feeling. 'And what is it with you and the snake? Money, I guess.'

'Yeah, I got a buyer.'

'Some zoo?'

'Who says zoo? It would be a big hassle to get this long fellow out of India. They like paperwork in this country. Very old-fashioned. Means a big, big bribe. No, I have found buyer here, not bother with import-export papers. That's where we're going now.'

'But why kidnap me? I'm no use to you . . .'

'Ah, that was just lucky break. You see, turn out that buyer is also interested in the Hunt family. So, kill two birds with one stone, to use an old Chinese proverb.'

'English, you mean. That's just like you to even steal a proverb.'

Frazer's mind was coming back into focus. Chung

liked to talk; it might be that he would let slip some piece of information that might save him.

'Who is this buyer?'

'Someone who wanted the snake very much. And someone who also was very interested to find out that the Hunts were chasing the same animal. He offered me even more money if I could bring back you and your old man. Too dangerous to tackle the old lion, but we got the cub, eh?'

And then, laughing his high-pitched laugh, Chung climbed through to the cab of the truck, and the journey continued right through the night and into the next day.

It was long, hot and uncomfortable. Frazer spent most of it lying next to the snake. He grew to dislike intensely the musty, heavy smell of the thing. And he was petrified that it might stir and wrap him again in an embrace that must this time be fatal.

'Steady, snaky,' he would say, and the snake would seem to settle down.

He did manage to sleep, drifting in and out of dreams, thinking at times that he was safely in his bed. There was no hope of escape. The four men in the back of the truck saw to that, not to mention the ropes binding him.

He tried speaking to them a couple of times. But either they couldn't speak English or they had orders not to communicate with him. Eventually, one – a

Filipino with a scar that ran from his scalp down to his chin – slid his finger across his throat in the universal language that said, 'If I were you, old chap, I'd quieten down.'

Once the snake did stir, and the bag over its head moved to and fro – almost as if the creature were trying to shake itself into wakefulness.

'Hey, fellas, you might want to check this out . . .' said Frazer, his voice rising in pitch, but one of the guards was already on it and sunk another syringe into the beast.

For the rest of that day, Frazer saw nothing of the outside world. He knew that he was still in India, but where was a mystery.

It was night again when the truck arrived at its destination. Frazer was bundled out as he'd been bundled in. He sensed the effort and tumult behind him when it was the turn of the snake to be removed from the truck. Chung's men passed him on to some rather more impressive specimens in uniforms and turbans. But they were no more friendly.

Chung himself made a brief appearance. He stood in front of Frazer and seemed to be about to say something. A word formed on his lips. Frazer thought it might have been 'sorry'. But then, whatever the word was, he scurried away without uttering it.

With his hands still tied, the new guards led him

down some stairs and thrust him into the dark interior of what looked a lot like a dungeon. In it there were cages, barely illuminated by a dim bulb, but it was enough to show him that he was not alone. There were two other figures in the cages: a man and a woman. They were holding hands through the bars.

His captors untied his hands, opened a door to one of the cages and pushed him in, locking the door behind him.

'Er, hi,' he said, for want of anything better. 'I, er, guess we're in the same fix.'

As the man came towards him into the light, he saw a face he'd only ever seen in photos, a face with the same strong jawline and glittering, intelligent eyes of his father.

'Well, I'll be . . .' the man said. Then he turned to the woman, who looked ill and drawn. 'Stand up, Ling-Mei, and meet your nephew, Frazer.'

'You're, you're . . .' stammered Frazer.

'Yep, Uncle Roger and Aunt Ling-Mei. And I'm sorry to see you here, young man.'

Ling-Mei staggered towards him.

'Amazon,' she said, 'Amazon, is she . . .?'

Frazer shook his head.

'She's safe and a long, long way from here,' he replied.

'And your dad?' There was hope in Roger Hunt's voice.

'He wasn't captured when I was. He's free, somewhere. And, if I know anything in the wide world is true, it's that he's on his way to find us.'

Roger smiled. 'Come sit down as close as you can,' he said. 'There's a lot of news we need to hear.'

'And I guess there's a few things you could tell me, as well,' said Frazer.

15

The Hunts Meet the Hunters

So, when Amazon Hunt cried out and ran to the bars of the cage and stretched her hands through to meet those of her mother, Ling-Mei and Roger Hunt were both horrified. They had thought her safe and sound, yet here she was, in the clutches of their greatest enemy.

'MUM!' said Amazon, but already her voice was thick with tears.

'No, no, no,' sobbed her mother. 'You should not be here.'

Amazon knew why her mother said these words. Her presence meant danger, possibly death. And yet she could see the conflicted expression on her mother's face. Her anguish could not quell the joy at seeing her only daughter again after so long.

Her father was in the next cage, and she stretched her other arm out so she could touch him too.

'I thought I'd never see you again . . .' Amazon said, sobbing, smiling, sobbing.

'If only it had been in some other place, some other way,' said Roger Hunt, entwining his fingers with hers.

'Hey, just ignore me, why dontcha,' came a voice from the other side.

Amazon looked up and saw Frazer. Now it was her turn to be both delighted to see someone and yet to wish fervently that they were not there.

'Well, what a delightful little scene. It's enough to make the heart melt.'

In the emotional swamp that had engulfed her, Amazon had totally failed to realize that the dismal cellar, stinking of animals, had filled up with people.

She spun round and saw the group who had been up in the main room of the lodge. Some of the guards were holding burning torches, which added their eerie, flickering glow to the dim electric light from the single bulb.

The man who spoke appeared strangely both old and ageless – his face was lined, but his wiry body was still vigorous. There was a knotty hump of muscle and sinew between his shoulder blades. His eyes were narrow slits, and his mouth was moist and red. There was something . . . *carnivorous* about him.

Amazon felt waves of malice, perhaps even evil, pulse from the man, like radiation from a damaged nuclear power station. And, without needing to be told, she knew who this was. It was the old enemy of her father and her uncle. It was . . .

'You're scum, Kaggs,' spat her father. 'And, like all scum, you're going to get wiped away.'

'Ho ho ho,' said the man called Kaggs, 'this is exactly the attitude, the *spirit*, I need. I was a little afraid that time might have dulled you, left you stooped and old and weary, Roger Hunt. And that would have been no fun at all. You were such a lively little fellow, always up to mischief. Always in trouble. I'm only sorry that your oaf of a brother is not here to complete the picture. It's so nice for a hunter to be able to bag a family group – a male, a female, a couple of cubs. Yes, that's the photo we all want.'

'Look, Kaggs,' said Roger Hunt, standing tall. 'You've got a beef with me and my brother going back to when we were kids. I know that. But these others here, my wife and daughter, and young Frazer, they're nothing to do with our old feud. Let them go and, when this is all over and you're in jail, I'll tell the authorities to go easy on you. I'll explain that you're a madman or a halfwit, whatever it takes to make them treat you leniently. Believe me, you don't want to spend your dying days in an Indian prison.'

Kaggs smiled. His teeth were grey and blunt and strong.

'Oh, if only it were that simple, Roger. Personally, I bear your spouse and your offspring no malice. But things have gone too far. Commerce is at stake. Money has been paid. The die is cast.'

'What are you blathering about, Kaggs? What is this . . .?'

'You know what it is, Roger. You see around me some of the world's richest men. Add to that the fact that they're all men who share a passion for the thrill of the hunt and we have a match made in heaven. Even something as exciting as killing gets boring in the end – shot one moose, shot them all. So I supply them with the rarest animals on the planet, to add a challenge and a touch of flavour to the killing. And when they heard that I had the famous Hunt family here – a family dedicated to spoiling their pleasure – well, they just had to come along to say . . . goodbye.

'So, let me introduce you to a few of my associates here.' He made an expansive gesture, covering the ten or so other men – not including the servants and guards – who had followed him into the cellar.

'Our dear friend the Maharaja you know already,' he said. 'Rich in land and property, with more palaces than he can use, but short on actual folding money.' Kaggs rubbed his fingers together, pulling a ludicrously crafty face. 'I like to think that we're partners in this enterprise.'

The Maharaja had the decency to look a little ashamed.

'And Doctor Drexler here, you know so very, very well.' Drexler had been lurking in the shadows, and they had all failed to spot him. 'I've helped to fund some of his more interesting . . . *experiments*, which will both advance the cause of science – I'm all for furthering human knowledge – *and* provide an extra bit of spice to my, or rather *our*, business.'

'Is this strictly necessary,' said Drexler who was looking faintly uncomfortable. His grey face carried a film of sweat.

'You're a filthy traitor,' yelled Frazer, gripping the bars of his cage with white-hot intensity. 'We trusted you. You were supposed to be my dad's friend. Well, you're going to find out that, if you double-cross the Hunts, you –'

Frazer never got any further. On some wordless signal from the Maharaja or Kaggs, a guard stepped forward and rapped his knuckles with one of the long sticks used for crowd control by the Indian police.

Frazer uttered a yelp of agony and nestled his damaged fingers in his armpit.

Drexler's eyes opened in surprise and, perhaps, disapproval at the violence, but he said nothing.

'That's quite enough of that,' said Kaggs. But it was clear he was talking about Frazer's outburst, not the brutality of the guard. 'Do be a good boy – I don't want to have to inflict any damage on you before the fun starts.'

Drexler shook his head, as if dealing with some inner spark of conscience for the first time. He appeared to be taking a great interest in his own feet all of a sudden.

'But now,' continued Kaggs, 'I must introduce you to my paying guests – without whom none of this would be possible. We have gathered together the world's best – which is to say wealthiest – big-game hunters. This,' he gestured to a fat, red-faced man Amazon recognized from the Maharaja's party, 'is Mr Laramie of Texas in the good old US of A.'

'Pleased to meet y'all,' said Laramie, a pleasant smile on his fleshy face.

'Mr Laramie might look and sound like the sort of character who would fire a Colt 45 pistol or a Winchester rifle, but I understand his preferred weapon is a Bushmaster .223 assault rifle, with the selector switched to full automatic. Am I right, Mr Laramie?'

'Finest gun money can buy,' smiled the American, showing a set of gleaming white teeth one could only possibly get through cosmetic surgery.

After that, to Amazon, the hunters began to blur together. There was a French aristocrat called Leconte, and a German called Herr Frapp, with skin so pale it was almost translucent, like a deep-sea fish brought to the surface. There were two more Americans, one a drug dealer with an Uzi, the other a Wall Street banker, who looked bored and impatient with the whole thing. There was a drawling English lord called Smethwyck, and an Australian media magnate called McKlintock, but Amazon had stopped listening. They were all, in their various ways, repellent.

The very last to be introduced was another that Amazon recognized from the Maharaja's palace. It was the tall, austere-looking African. He remained back in the shadows, as if too important to have to engage with the prisoners.

'And here is Chief Amunda Banda,' said Kaggs, 'who has managed to cream off millions of pounds of aid money intended to help the poor in his own country. Well, good I say. They'd only waste it on luxuries like food and clothes. I'm hoping to see the good chief use a spear before the fun is over. How about it, chief?'

The African said nothing, but merely bowed. His face showed no emotion and was as unreadable as one of the burnt pages in Roger Hunt's diary.

'Well, your family has been a thorn in the side of these men for too long. We were put on this Earth as the most intelligent of species, my friends. It is our instinct, our role, our nature to hunt and gather. We shouldn't be ashamed to hang the heads of our kills on our walls as trophies. That is how we truly show respect for those creatures we conquer. In the same way we have for millennia. Needless to say, no one here will shed a tear at the demise of you and that excuse for an organization you call TRACKS.

'Now, gentlemen. You have a busy day ahead of you tomorrow, so, if you wouldn't mind leaving us to make your final preparations, I'd like to have a last little private talk with my old compadre and his family.'

The hunters, guided by the servants, filed back out of the cellar.

'Alone at last!' said Kaggs, stepping closer to the cages. Amazon could smell him now. It was a harsh, musky smell, only partially obscured by cologne and whisky. She could tell that he was enjoying every moment of this long-anticipated revenge.

'But let me tell you a little more,' he continued, 'about the set-up here. As you may know, we are in the cellars of the grand hunting lodge built by the Maharaja's illustrious great-grandfather. It sits in the middle of his hunting estate, which has been here for very much longer. We are surrounded by ten thousand acres of the most varied and rich ecosystems in the whole of India. We have, within the boundaries of the estate, prime dense jungle, open forest, savannah, a noble river. It's like a perfect world, a little Eden, ripe for . . . violation.

'It has been stocked – with great help, I might say, from TRACKS,' he nodded generously at Drexler, who continued to look down – 'with animals mainly, of course, from India, but also from the wider world. We have tigers and leopards, naturally, but also zebra, the saiga antelope that my old friend Roger was studying out in central Asia. We have those charming near relations of ours, the chimps and gorillas, and orang-utans. The rarer the better, of course, which is why we also have a few giant pandas, sweet fluffy darlings that they are.'

'You beast!' exclaimed Amazon, unable to keep quiet any longer.

'Beast? Well, we're all beasts under our clothes, my dear,' replied Kaggs in a friendly way.

16

Chung Chained

At that moment they were interrupted by a violent commotion. For a happy second or two, Amazon thought that perhaps it was Hal Hunt, arriving to rescue them with a platoon of local police.

But then she recognized the voice. It was one she had, in the past, feared and loathed.

'What is this ten thousand dollar? Promise was million dollar. You got big snake, you got boy. Chung wants million dollar, like promise!'

All eyes turned to the figure who had bustled down into the cellar. He was struggling with the tall, moustachioed guards, trying to break free of their grip. He bit one and kicked at the shins of another.

'Bring him here,' said Kaggs in a low voice that was full of menace.

The guards threw the Chinese smuggler at his feet.

Chung struggled to his knees, still gabbling about the money.

'I gotta pay my men. They good men, not cheap . . .'

But then Kaggs, without another word, walked over and kicked him in the stomach.

Suddenly the cellar became utterly silent. Kaggs loomed over the fallen man, and Amazon saw he had a pistol in his hand.

'I told you to kill them all or bring them all back here. All you've done is leave a trail for the most dangerous man I know. He will, unless I am much mistaken, come looking. This has put my organization in jeopardy. By rights I should have killed you on the spot. I let my generous nature get the better of me, and offered you enough so that you broke even. Now what is broken is my patience.'

He thumbed off the safety catch and pointed the pistol at Chung's head.

Chung didn't seem to understand what was happening. He stared at the barrel of the gun as if he'd never seen anything like it before. The Hunts looked on in horrified silence. Kaggs was going to murder this man, right before their eyes.

And then Kaggs appeared to change his mind. A smile again played over his lips.

'I've got a better idea. You can keep our friends the Hunts company until morning. Then I'll come back and kill you all, after you've spent the next eight hours marinating in your own misery and defeat.

And put the brat in with her mother. Only a monster would deny them a last night together.'

'No!' screamed Chung. 'Not fair! Not fair!'

But Kaggs wasn't listening. He had already gone.

The guards thrust Chung into the empty cage at the end. It wasn't easy – he clung to the bars around the door, and his fingers had to be prised open. When he was finally in and the door locked, he squatted in the corner and stared at the ground.

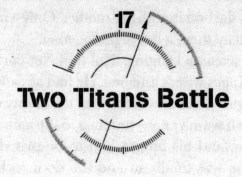

17
Two Titans Battle

She was hungry now. And confused. Nothing that had happened to her in the past hours was understandable. She had been in her own jungle, its smells and sounds so familiar. But now she was here, in this other place, and she didn't know how or why.

That situation could not be helped, but something could certainly be done about the hunger.

She tasted the warm air with her tongue. Oh yes, there was something out there. The taste was strong. She moved silently through the thick undergrowth, each rhythmic undulation taking her closer. It was dark, too dark to see, but she didn't need vision on this hunt. And now she was close enough to use another of her senses. Little pits lined her upper lip. They allowed her to 'see' heat, like an infra-red camera.

There were five of them. Three big ones. Two smaller. Their outlines were clear to her, warm and red against the cooler background. One of the big ones was very big indeed. She would avoid that one. But yes, a smaller one was separate from the others. She moved closer again. It was sitting hunched over, intent on its meal of fruit.

She felt the powerful digestive juices in her long, long gut begin to flow. She was so close now her senses were crackling and fizzing. The smell, the taste and the heat that she saw were like hot waves of fire.

And then her other sense – the hearing that was really a feeling of vibrations – pinged awake. Something was hurtling towards her. Something big and powerful that made the ground beneath her shake as it approached.

The big male gorilla, silver-backed and magnificent, had heard the rustle as the snake moved over the forest floor. He had encountered big snakes before, back in Africa, but nothing quite like this. It was as long as a tree, and he sensed the power beneath the scaly skin. But that didn't matter. His job was a simple one – to protect his family.

He knew that he should have had them safely up in the trees by now, but he hadn't been himself since their ordeal – the capture by the men with the guns that fired stinging darts resulting in long sleeps. Everything in this forest was different – the plants, the animals, the smells and tastes. And he had been ashamed that he'd let them be taken here. But now his moment had come.

He bellowed out a roar that was both a war cry and a warning to his family, and then charged at the snake as it was preparing to strike at the little two-year-old female.

He grabbed the snake in his strong hands and tried to bring it to his powerful jaws. But the snake threw a coil round the gorilla's neck and began to tighten. Another coil wound round the gorilla's legs. But then, with a great shudder, the gorilla expanded its

mighty chest and shrugged free of the python. At last it got the chance to bite. It was a bite that would have broken the back of a leopard. And then the gorilla lifted the snake above its head and hurled it away.

The snake didn't go very far – it was simply too heavy, too long and awkward a shape, but the bite, behind her head, had hurt her. Her scales gave her some protection, as did her sheer size, and meant the gorilla's jaws couldn't exert their full force, but that did not take away the deep unpleasantness of the experience. This was not what she had expected. There was nothing like this black hairy creature in her own jungle. It was not a fight she relished. And so she slithered away, leaving the triumphant male gorilla and his startled family behind.

She would find easier pickings soon enough.

18

Night Visitor

Amazon was on the hard stone floor of the cage. Her mother was next to her, holding her in an embrace so fierce it might almost have been an attack. Amazon's mind had been full of the horror of what Kaggs had just told them – that they were to be held for a night and then slaughtered like animals, but now it was flooded with love and warmth. They had at least this last night together. And they filled the first part of it with talk.

Ling-Mei told the story of their discovery of Kaggs's vast scheme, of their flight across Asia and Canada and the small explosion that brought them down, caused by a device planted by Kaggs's agents. It had been Roger's idea to stay in hiding in the wilderness, making Kaggs believe that they were dead. He planned to return secretly to TRACKS HQ to give the whole story to Hal, but then Kaggs's men had finally found them and brought them, after a long and terrible journey, to this place.

'I think his plan was to get us together here – Roger, Hal, me, you and Frazer – and kill us all. It was just a terrible sick revenge for all the times the boys had got the better of him back when they were young.'

And then Amazon almost lost control. 'But he *has* beaten us,' she cried. 'We're trapped here and there's no way out, and, except for Uncle Hal, we're all going to –'

'Don't say it,' said Frazer.

Amazon looked up at him, thinking he was just putting a brave face on their situation. But then she saw where he was looking. Amazon could sense that her father was up to something. She peered through the gloom of the dungeon, trying to make out what he was doing. He appeared to be working away at one of the old metal bars to the cage. He almost seemed to be sawing, but it looked to Amazon as though he were sawing with thin air. Had her father gone mad? Then she caught a faint smell in the dank air of the dungeon.

Something . . . *minty*.

'Dad, what are you doing?' she whispered, curiosity taking over, momentarily, from the fear and desolation she was feeling.

He looked up. The sweat glistened on his forehead.

'I managed to persuade Kaggs's guards to leave us with a few scraps of civilization. Including these.'

Roger held up some dental floss and a tube of toothpaste.

'I remembered reading somewhere about an Italian Mafia boss who'd used dental floss to cut through the bars of a prison he was being held in. It seemed worthwhile giving it a go.'

'But surely it can't work?' said Amazon, squeezing as close as she could to try to see. 'I mean, *floss* . . .'

And now she did see the thin white line of the dental floss – and, amazingly, it had cut through more than half of the bar.

'It's actually tougher than you think. The toothpaste helps to lubricate it, so the floss doesn't fray.'

'Uncle Roger, you're a genius,' said Frazer.

'I wouldn't go that far,' said Roger. 'But I'm damned if I'm going to let that madman kill my family. Now another few minutes and I may be able to kick through this bar, and then –'

Amazon's father was silenced by a scraping noise coming from the far wall of the cellar. And then, to their astonishment, they saw a trapdoor swing open from the floor and a head appear. Amazon's heart was in her mouth as she thought it was a guard coming to check on them. In the next cage, her father had clearly assumed the same. He was trying desperately to hide what he was doing, but the floss snagged in the cut he had made in the bar. Toothpaste foamed around it. The guard would be sure to see.

And then the weak light in the cellar fell on the face of the man. When Amazon saw who it was, she felt as though she could burst with joy and a smile lit up her face. It was the mute servant who had tried to help her back at the Maharaja's palace.

'It's OK, it's OK,' she gasped, 'I know this man.'

'And so,' said her father, 'do I. 'Hello, Mehmet, my old friend. It's been many, many years.'

The mute servant – Mehmet – bowed at Roger, and made some incomprehensible sounds with his ruined mouth.

Roger Hunt looked at him strangely. 'Mehmet, what's the matter?'

'Dad, he's lost his tongue,' said Amazon. 'It was probably the nasty little Maharaja.'

Her father spoke some words in broken Hindi to Mehmet, who was already opening the cages, one by one, with a heavy set of keys.

Then Mehmet signalled them urgently to follow him.

'What about me?' came a voice from the shadows. It was Chung. They'd completely forgotten about him.

'Let him rot,' said Frazer. 'He tried to kill us in Polynesia.'

'Not true!' squealed Chung. 'I'm just a businessman. I never kill anyone that didn't deserve it.'

'We haven't got time for this,' said Amazon's father. 'Let him go, Mehmet. He can come along with us until we're out of here, then we'll think again.'

Mehmet unlocked Chung, and then led them all back down through the trapdoor.

'Mehmet's been here for many years,' said Roger Hunt. 'I suppose he must know all the secrets of the place . . .'

There were crumbling wooden steps that took them down to a passageway. Mehmet had a weak torch, which shone its feeble light ahead, and they followed. The passage was short – mercifully, as even Amazon had to duck her head to avoid scraping it on whatever horrible creatures were living in the roof. In less than five minutes they emerged into a small ornamental garden at the back of the hunting lodge.

It was around midnight and there were still sounds of revelry from within – German drinking songs, bellows of coarse laughter, the clinking of glasses.

Mehmet put his finger to his mute lips – although none of them needed to be told that silence was crucial at that moment. They followed him in a crouching run across an area of open ground, until they reached the cover of some scrubby bushes. They gathered together, and Mehmet thrust a few sheets of paper into Frazer's hands. Amazon could see that, as well as some written notes, there was a map.

Mehmet lit an old metal lighter, and Amazon's father read out the message.

'My old friend Roger and Mrs Roger and

Children, follow this map to get to Temple place. At the Temples you can find a place of some safety from the wild beasts of the night. It is possible that you can hide there for long time. Or follow on map direction to river. Might be able escape across, but crocodile many. Cannot go over wall – on top of old stone has been put deadly electric!!! And also many camera there. I will try to go through gate, as I am trusted and known to guard. Maharaja cut out tongue, so I can never speak his secrets, but I learned to read and write. Will find brother Hal, bring here.'

Then Mehmet pointed in the direction they must follow and made shooing motions.

'Thank you, Mehmet, my friend,' said Roger. 'And if we get through this I'll make sure you have a safe job at TRACKS.'

Mehmet touched his head, bowed and scurried away.

'OK, guys,' said Roger. 'We've got to get to this temple as soon as we can. The map says north. Is that one of those fancy TRACKS compass watches I see on your wrist, Frazer?'

'It sure as heck is.'

'Then lead on!'

19

The Temple Trek

The trek through the forest night was difficult and dangerous. There was just enough starlight for them to see each other, and to pick a slow path between the trees. Occasionally the moon would come out from behind a cloud and they would get a sense of the vastness around them. But it was impossible not to blunder into hanging vines or trip over roots. Frazer and Roger led the way, followed by Amazon and Ling-Mei, hand in hand.

Chung trudged at the back, muttering and grumbling to himself.

Frazer knew all too well the dangers of walking like this, unseeing, through unknown territory. On every other mission he'd been on, the rule was to camp at night, to light a fire, to huddle close. Night was the time of predators. And they all knew that no other forest in the world contained as many potential killers as this. But, as ever, it was the bugs that Frazer complained about.

'OK, that's it, I'm devoting the rest of my life to developing an anti-bug spray that satellites could deliver from space and wipe out every single blasted mosquito on the planet.'

He slapped ineffectually at his neck.

'And what about all the birds and animals that eat the mosquitoes?' said Ling-Mei, smiling in the darkness.

'Yeah, I know. Circle of life and all that stuff. But why do they always eat me alive? Zonnie hardly ever gets bit – OW!'

'What is it now, Fraze?' said Amazon.

'Some plant just stung the heck out of my face. I'm really going off India in a big way. Jeepers, it burns.'

Roger and Ling-Mei gathered round.

'Don't move,' said Ling-Mei. 'You've walked into a creeper of some kind.'

She pulled her sleeve down over her hand and moved some vines away from Frazer's face.

'It really hurts,' said Frazer.

'Did it get in your eyes?' asked Ling-Mei urgently.

'No . . . I don't think so, just my face.'

Ling-Mei peered at the leaves in the murk.

'I think it's a member of the genus *Tragia* – commonly called a noseburn.'

'Well, that's got it right, because my nose and the rest of my face feel like they're burning off.'

'Is it bad?' asked Amazon, suddenly concerned.

She'd got used to Frazer's half-playful complaining, but this seemed serious.

'We need to wash the skin. The noseburn has prickles that inject a rubbery sap. That's what's causing the burning sensation. It can be very nasty if we don't get it clean . . . Anyone got any water?' she asked, though it seemed a futile hope – none of them had any bottled water, and they hadn't heard any streams in the dry woods.

'Got this,' said a sulky voice. 'Idiots not even search Chung before they put him in cage like animal.'

He held out a bottle to Ling-Mei.

'What is it?'

'Medicine. Good stuff.'

Ling-Mei took the bottle, unscrewed the lid and had a sniff.

'Gin!'

'Take it or leave it, lady. Myself, I'd rather drink it than waste on boy's face. But the longer we stand around hear gossiping, sooner we get caught and shot by Kaggs . . . or worse, eaten alive!'

Ling-Mei shrugged. 'Better than nothing. OK, Frazer, close your eyes. This is going to sting.' Then she poured the gin all over his face.

Frazer really wanted to scream. It was like she'd fired a flame-thrower at his face. He clenched his hands, and found that he was gripping other hands – the hands of Amazon and his Uncle Roger.

It was Roger who said, 'You got it, Fraze. You're

as tough as your dad, and he's made out of tungsten steel and depleted uranium.'

To Frazer's surprise, the gin seemed to work.

'Hey, it's feeling better,' he said after a few seconds.

'I knew it would,' said Chung. 'Still, would rather have been drinking nice gin and tonic watching sun set into sea back home. So maybe now we move?'

Frazer checked the compass, the luminous dial green in the starlight, and moved on.

20
Black and White

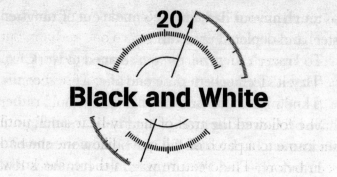

Her ambush site – a patch of dead reeds by a dry stream bed – had proved ill-judged. Nothing suitable had come within striking range. A small herd of elephants had passed by, shying away from her scent, but even a baby elephant was too big a mouthful for her.

Smaller prey – black rats and an angry porcupine – had ambled or scurried by. But the rats were too small to be of interest, and the porcupine, although succulent beneath the spines, was not a relaxing meal. She had a distant memory of a porcupine charging backwards at her, leaving an agonizing deposit of spines in her face. After the encounter with the gorilla, she wanted easy meat: deer, or antelope, or gazelle.

And so she moved on, slowly, silently, through the forest.

She picked up a scent. Again it was new, but, unlike with the gorilla, it was vaguely familiar. The scent reminded her a little of bear. Well, she had eaten bear before. Not a full-grown one perhaps, but a cub, or even a juvenile . . . yes, that would go down very well. There were dangers, of course, but she was hungry, very hungry.

She followed the trail of nearly-bear-smell until she came to a patch of tall grass, like none she had seen before. The creature was in there, she knew. Slowly, slowly, she crawled. The moon came out from behind a cloud and she saw through the thick stems of the bamboo the sleeping form of the bear. She knew it was a bear by the shape, but its colouring of white and black was most unbearlike. The weird pattern broke up the outline of the creature and also confused her. It made it hard for her to judge its size. She came closer, curious.

It was big. But was it *too* big?

Well, there was one way to find out. The panda – a fully-grown female – snuffled in its sleep, unaware of the grisly fate that awaited it.

The python pulled back, preparing to strike, the huge muscles that ran along its supple spine thrumming with energy and anticipation.

And then she sensed the vibration in the ground. Feet. Lots of feet. They were close. She flicked out her tongue and caught the hated scent of humans. She looked into the moonshadowed forest and saw them. They were trying to be stealthy, but her senses found them. There were big humans – she had learned to be wary of those. But there were also smaller ones, not quite cubs, not quite adults.

She thought again about the strange bear. Bears had claws and teeth. And so she left the panda to its dreams of bamboo and moved stealthily after Roger, Ling-Mei, Amazon and Frazer Hunt, and the skulking Chung.

21

Kaggs Thwarted

Merlin Kaggs was not a man to waste the opportunity to torment his enemies. He had enjoyed a fine meal, but now he wanted a proper . . . *dessert*.

And so, as the hunters were drifting off into drunken sleep, he nodded curtly to the guard at the cellar door, who bowed and unlocked it. Kaggs padded down the stairs, rehearsing the things he would say, the quips and taunts. Yet, almost as soon as he entered the dark space, he knew that it was empty, and that he had been betrayed.

He walked over to the cages.

'Well, well, well,' he said to himself. 'It seems our guests decided not to stay the night.'

At an earlier stage of his criminal career he might have raged and raved, spitting, punching the walls, cursing. But he had learned to control his emotions. And that control, allied to his native cunning and his utter ruthlessness, had made him a rich man. A man wealthy enough – with the aid of that old popinjay the Maharaja – to put into operation his long-planned revenge against the Hunts.

He wasn't really going to have them shot in the morning. That would be a waste. He was going to wait until he had captured the other one – the one he hated more than all the others combined. And then, when he had them all . . . well, that's when the fun would start.

But now it seemed that his prey had escaped. He paced across the floor, and soon found the outline of the trapdoor. He crouched down, took out his knife and prised it open, and looked into the deeper darkness of the tunnel.

'Run all you like, Hunts,' he said, in a low, even voice. 'I'm going to catch you and kill you. Slowly. That's if one of your precious animals doesn't get to you first.'

Then he stood upright once more, leaving the trapdoor wide open, and walked briskly back up the stairs. A few snapped commands to the servants and the millionaires were soon assembled in the great hall, some bleary-eyed, some angry at being disturbed.

'What the heck is this?' said someone – the drug dealer and gangster, whose name was Big Zee. Kaggs gave him his best black-eyed stare and silence descended.

'Gentlemen,' said Kaggs, 'I have a new entertainment planned for tomorrow. It seems that we have a traitor in our midst and that, as a consequence, our birds have flown the coop. I need not tell you how . . . *awkward* it would be for us if our enterprise here were to be discovered by the authorities. It's important that we catch up with those people and deal with them . . . *permanently*. But there's no reason why this shouldn't be fun. You're hunters, and tomorrow morning, as dawn breaks, we hunt the Hunts.'

The American banker said, 'What if they get away? Why the heck don't we start after them now?'

Some of those in the great hall shouted their assent. Others were quieter, as they thought of their comfortable beds. Some may have been uneasy about the idea of hunting humans, but, if they were, they concealed what they feared might be considered a sign of weakness.

'There's no need,' said Kaggs. He turned to the Maharaja, who was wearing an ornate dressing gown made of red silk with golden embroidery. 'I assume you have a skilled guide we can send out after them . . .? When he finds them, he can radio back their position. We can be out there in the jeeps in no time. Much better than blundering about in the dark. That's for the quarry. We are the hounds.'

'Well, my best tracker is certainly Mehmet,' replied the Maharaja. 'But I'm afraid he couldn't radio back with any information, as I was forced to remove his . . . that is to say, a minor operation was performed on him to ensure his, ah, discretion. Actually, I haven't seen the scallywag in quite some time . . .'

When a brief search failed to find Mehmet, and a report came back from the gatehouse that he'd been seen leaving the compound, on, it was said, 'important business for the Maharaja', Kaggs declared, 'Well, it seems we have our traitor. Maharaja, dispatch some of your best men to find him. I want him brought back to me before he does any damage. I will personally remove his skin.'

The Maharaja looked most offended. 'Dear chap,' he said, 'that will not do. He's been my servant for forty years. If anyone is to skin him alive, it is I.'

'As you wish. Anyway, send your best tracker – I mean, your best tracker *with a tongue* – after the Hunts. I need to know where they are.'

And so it was that another of the Maharaja's men set out into the forest night to find the fugitives, and the millionaires returned to their beds, to dream of the excitement of the day ahead.

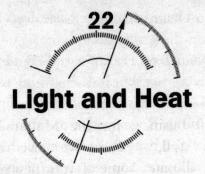

22

Light and Heat

'I think we're here,' said Roger Hunt. 'The temple complex. This is where Mehmet thought it might be safe to rest for a while.'

And they certainly needed the rest. It wasn't just that they hadn't slept, or that the trek had been tiring – although exhaustion certainly played a role – it was more the fact that they were constantly on the alert for night stalkers. Every crackling twig or strange call in the night made their adrenalin surge, as their bodies prepared for fight or flight. Twice they heard roars – 'Lion,' said Ling-Mei the first time, 'Tiger,' the second. Then there were the eerie barks and yelps, and other sounds like the wails of torture victims.

Frazer looked around. And yes, there did seem to be strange structures surrounding them. In the starlight all he could do was sense their rough outlines, but he got a distinct impression of . . . majesty.

'This must have been some place, back in the day,' he said.

'How's your face, Fraze?' asked Amazon.

'Uh, ugly as ever. But it doesn't sting too bad any more. I guess Chung's magic medicine did the trick.'

'OK, Chung,' Roger said to the animal smuggler. 'Now we've got away from the immediate danger, you've got a choice. You can clear off and take your chances out there on your own. Or you can stay and help us all get out of this.'

'No, Dad!' yelled Amazon. She couldn't believe that her father had made this offer to Chung. It was bad enough that he was with them even for this first part of the journey. But for him to stay with them was unthinkable. 'You don't know what he's like. He tried to kill Frazer and me . . . he's not . . . stable.'

'Amazon,' her father said patiently, his hands on her shoulders, his eyes looking deeply into hers, 'I know exactly what kind of man Mr Chung is. We've been tracking his activities for years. He's greedy and sly and he'll do whatever it takes to earn money. But, whatever you might think from his play-acting, he's no fool and he knows how to handle himself in a fight. And we need every soldier we have if we're going to get out of this alive. And remember, this isn't just about us. Kaggs has stocked this place full of rare animals. If we don't make it, they won't either. So, Chung, what do you say – fight with us or die out there alone?'

Chung's eyes moved rapidly round the group, and then out into the jungle beyond them. Amazon could almost hear his brain working. Would he be better off alone, skulking, letting the bigger party attract all the attention from the hunters, human and animal? Or should he throw his lot in with them?

And then Ling-Mei Hunt astonished everyone by taking two quick steps towards Chung and delivering a punch to his chin that left him sitting on the jungle floor, looking even more perplexed than before.

'That's for hurting my little girl,' she said, her mouth tight with fury. 'And, if you ever harm a member of my family again, I'll make you wish you'd never left that rat-infested fishing village in the Philippines.'

And then she spat a few more choice words at Chung in Chinese.

'OK, crazy lady, you make your point. I'll stay and help. One for all, all for one.'

Frazer couldn't help but smile. 'Well, Aunt Ling-Mei, remind me never to get on the wrong side of you!'

23

Shelter

More by touch than by sight, they found an ancient temple building that seemed to offer some protection. It was roofless, but still had the remains of four walls. The forest had grown in and around it, so the stone of the walls seemed to belong more to the world of nature than the world of humans.

'We can build a fire here without being seen,' said Roger. 'And it'll be easier to defend against men or animals. You know how to light a fire, Frazer?'

'Yep, if I've got the tools. I usually use a firesteel and my knife . . . Wait, knife! Those dumb schmucks never even bothered to search me cos I'm a kid, I guess, but look, I've still got my pocketknife!'

'Well,' said Roger, 'that's going to come in mighty handy. But how will it help us light a fire, without the steel?'

'Hmmm, well, if we had some flint . . .'

'No flint here, Frazer. What other ways are there of starting a fire?'

Frazer concentrated. He knew all this stuff, but his mind had gone blank. He felt like he was representing his dad in some ancient contest between the two brothers. But all he could think of was rubbing two sticks together, like some kind of halfwit. But at least the sticks got him thinking along the right lines.

'Well, there's the flat board and stick method. Only . . . well, I've tried that many times and my arm always gets tired from rubbing the hardwood stick up and down the groove in the softwood long before there's any hint of an ember.'

'Not just you, young man. I haven't ever managed to start a fire that way, either.'

That admission gave Frazer more confidence. In fact, later, Frazer wondered if Uncle Roger had said it for that very reason, and that he'd actually been starting fires all his life in exactly that way.

'OK, then a better way is the bow drill method.'

Roger Hunt nodded. 'Yep, that's what I'd go for. So what do we need?'

'Er, a bow and a drill, for a start. Then the softwood for the bottom, the what-d'you-call-it, er, fireboard, that's it, and some hardwood for the top section.'

'I usually find a rock is best for that – especially if it's a nice soft rock like sandstone, that you can dig a notch in. And what do you plan to use for cordage?'

'Cordage?'

'The string, for the bow.'

'Oh, I hadn't thought of that. Er, I know you can twist together plant fibres. Me and Amazon made some pretty good rope by doing that with coconut fibres on a desert island . . .'

'See any coconuts?' Roger smiled.

'No, but there must be something else . . .'

'Your Aunt Ling-Mei can make cord out of just about anything. But me, I like the easy way. Take your boots off.'

'What? Oh.' And then Frazer started laughing. 'My bootlaces! Of course.'

Ten minutes later, they had collected everything they needed from the area in and around the ruins. It helped that the moon had finally risen beyond the last of the clouds and cast its quicksilver light over the scene.

Roger had found an old splintered branch of cedar wood, and wrenched it apart to form the fireboard. He used Frazer's pocketknife to cut a notch in it, and then scraped a little pile of bark from the outside, and set it neatly a few centimetres from the notch. Then he cut and trimmed a piece from the edge to form the spindle – the 'arrow' to go with the bow. The bow itself was a stout twig, as thick as Frazer's finger. Roger bent it, and tied Frazer's shoelace to each end with a simple knot. Then Roger twisted the spindle in the shoelace, so the lace formed a loop around it.

As Frazer watched his uncle completing their

preparations, he couldn't help but compare Roger with his dad. Hal Hunt was a powerful man, with short, strong fingers that seemed indestructible. They were impervious to heat – Frazer had seen him pick up pans from the fire that even ten minutes later were too hot for Frazer to touch. Roger's fingers were longer – they looked more used to playing the piano than making fires – but Frazer could see the intelligence in them, and a steely, springy strength.

When Roger had finished, he handed the bow and spindle set-up to Frazer.

'Really, me?' said Frazer, looking amazed and flattered.

'Sure. You know what you're doing, I can tell that.'

Frazer arranged the bow and spindle so that the tip of the arrow was in the notch. Then Roger pressed firmly down on top of it with a flattened piece of sandstone wrenched from the wall. Frazer began to move the bow backwards and forwards, which made the spindle spin. Or it should have done.

'Too much friction,' said Frazer, getting frustrated.

'How clean are your ears, son?' asked Roger, smiling his slow smile again.

'Huh? Well, not too clean I guess – haven't had a shower for a couple of days. Can't quite see how it matters, though, what with us about to be hunted down by a bunch of psychopaths and all . . .'

'Wax,' said Roger, hardly able to stop himself from laughing. 'The perfect lubricant for the top of the spindle. Have a good dig into your ear and see what you can find.'

Now Frazer joined in with the laughter as he rooted around in his ears.

They'd sent Chung out to gather firewood, and he came back at that moment carrying a fairly meagre armful.

'Mad Yankees,' was all he could think to say, seeing the man and the boy helpless with laughter, as the boy stuck his finger in his ear.

And the strange thing is that it worked. Frazer got just enough wax out of his ears to lubricate the spindle. The bow now worked perfectly, and in no more than thirty seconds they had first smoke, then a tiny hot cinder that caught in the dust created by the drilling. Roger moved it deftly to the shavings of bark, breathing life into it with infinite care.

Once the red eye of hope was set in the shavings, he blew a little more firmly, and smoke was soon billowing out. Frazer added a few twigs to the growing mini-inferno, and quickly real fingers of flame flickered out into the darkness.

In another minute, the branches brought by Chung had been carefully arranged around the flames and the fire was made.

There was nothing to eat – it was far too dark and dangerous to forage – but Chung passed round the bottle.

'Don't worry, crazy lady,' he said when he saw

Ling-Mei's fierce face in the flames. 'I saw a stream. Cleaned out bottle. Water not so nice, but better than nothing.'

There was enough for a swallow or two each. The water, muddy and gritty, still tasted good to Frazer. He hadn't realized just how thirsty he was.

24

Midnight Snack

She was not really designed for travelling long distances, but eventually she caught up with the humans. She tasted them in the air long before she reached the place; she also tasted the smoke. She didn't like that, but her hunger was driving her on. She was twenty metres away from the ruined temple when she detected another presence. First she felt the tiny vibrations in the earth caused by careful footsteps. And then she caught the new scent. Human again, but this time uncontaminated by the nasty fire.

She moved towards it, the rough scales of her belly gripping the dry earth and inching her forward.

And there, in the moonlight, she saw him.

The human, like her, was now lying on his belly. He had something in his hands. Of course she didn't recognize it, but it was a mobile phone. The keypad gave off a low green light. He punched in the digits, focused on what he was doing. It was perfect, so perfect.

She struck, her jaws closing round the man's upper body. His eyes burned white for a moment of intense shock and terror. He opened his mouth to scream, but only the first strangled syllable emerged before her coils were around him.

At last she had her meal.

25
Planning Ahead

'What the hell was that?'

Frazer sat bolt upright. They had all begun to drift off in the warmth of the fire. Amazon was nestled between her parents, their comforting presence better than any blanket.

Roger was on his feet in an instant.

'It was human, I think. Give me your knife, Fraze.'

Frazer handed it over.

'Thanks. Wait here.'

'Be careful, Dad,' said Amazon.

'I'm coming,' said Chung, surprising everyone. 'Can't sleep with all snoring from Hunts. Like living in zoo.'

Roger looked at him and nodded his assent.

As they went out through the broken doorway in the ruined wall, Frazer instinctively began to follow. Ling-Mei put her hand on his shoulder. She shook her head.

'They know what they're doing,' she said. 'You

stay here. After all, who else will look after me and Amazon?'

Frazer, Amazon and Ling-Mei didn't have to wait long for the other two to return.

'What was it, Dad?' asked Amazon. Then she saw that they were carrying some objects.

'There was nothing there,' said Roger. 'I mean, no one there. But we found these.' He held out a broken mobile phone and a gun.

'Does the phone work?' asked Ling-Mei hopefully.

'No. But the gun's OK. And that could be the difference between life and death out here.'

'It was probably scout,' said Chung.

'So what happened to him?' asked Frazer.

'Oh, he got eat. Lots here to do eating. Probably eat you, too, before long. We gotta go.'

'So what's the plan?' asked Frazer.

'Well,' said Roger, 'this means they know we've gone. I thought we'd have until the morning. Who knows how many men Kaggs will have out here, looking for us?'

He opened out the roughly drawn map that Mehmet had given him, and everyone gathered round.

'This big horseshoe shape here is the wall. And here's the river. We're in the middle, here, in the temple ruins. The hunting lodge is here, halfway to the front gate. The way I see it, we've got two choices – either we try to hide out until Hal finds us.

There's at least a chance that Mehmet might be able to get through. The trouble is that Kaggs's men will be looking, too, and we don't know if that scout managed to get a message out before . . . before whatever happened to him. I know Hal will turn up, I just can't guarantee that we'll still be alive when he does.'

'Not just Kaggs's men,' said Chung. 'I have bad feeling about those others – the killers. I think they might enjoy hunting ultimate prey . . .'

The others all looked at him, their faces incredulous, doubtful, horrified.

'You can't be serious,' said Frazer.

Chung shrugged. 'Getting killed is not something I joke about.'

'OK,' said Amazon, 'maybe we should assume the worst. And we've still got plan B – the river.'

'That's our best bet,' said Roger. 'We could try the wall, but Mehmet thought it was a no-no. And that gateway is too heavily defended for us the break out there. The only way is the river. We travelled about seven kilometres last night and, if this map is to scale, it looks to be about another fifteen on to the river. That shouldn't take us more than three hours, even over rough ground.'

Frazer was looking a little queasy.

'I, er, I really don't much care for crocs,' he said. 'Nothing much scares me in the animal world, but I just don't like the idea of one of those things dragging me down into the murky depths, and waiting till I drown, then tearing chunks off me by doing that death spin thing.'

Roger patted Frazer's shoulder. 'Believe me,' he said, 'I won't let any croc mess with my nephew. I've had run-ins with the kind of croc that would eat those muggers for breakfast – the saltwater crocs of New Guinea. Some of those boys are nearly seven metres long, and they'd as soon dine on humans as anything else, whereas the muggers aren't real maneaters usually. No, if all that's stopping us really are those crocs then we've got a chance. Muggers are nasty, but they're not the smartest creatures in the world. If we can find some carrion – something big, a buffalo, maybe – and dump it downriver, that should draw all the local crocs away and we can swim across.'

'Hah!' said Chung, who had been listening carefully. The Hunts all looked at him, expecting him to say something else. Frazer thought that he was going to express his doubts about their chances, but he said nothing more.

When it was obvious nothing audible was actually going to emerge from those narrow lips, Roger continued. 'OK, let's get moving. We'll find breakfast on the way.'

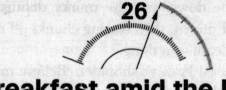

26

Breakfast amid the Ruins

The pale pre-dawn light was spreading slowly over the forest as the Hunts and Chung began the next stage of their journey.

Amazon looked around her. It had been impossible to appreciate their surroundings the night before, but now she was almost overwhelmed by it. They were in the sort of jungle you only ever seem to see in films: it was rich with huge hardwood trees, reaching a hundred metres into the sky. In between the towering monsters were smaller trees, and Amazon saw the deep yellows and reds and oranges of ripe bananas and mangoes. Vines reached down from the branches like dreadlocks, and small flocks of bright green parakeets zoomed from tree to tree. And then, stalking through the forest floor, she caught sight of the iridescent dazzle of a peacock's tail.

It was almost too much beauty to bear. And yet,

for once, the natural beauty was not what caught the eye.

Everywhere there were the remains of once great buildings, half toppled among the trees. Amazon saw what looked like stepped pyramids, crumbling into rubble. There were walls that looked like they may have belonged to great temples, and columns and arches standing alone, the ceilings they once supported long since fallen. On one wall she saw countless images carved into the stone. She couldn't quite see what they were in the murk, but they unsettled her and gave off a vague atmosphere of evil.

'Pretty cool, huh?' said Frazer. 'I wonder what happened to this place. I mean, why would you desert something as awesome as this?'

He'd been speaking to Amazon, but it was Chung who answered.

'War. Big kings fighting about ladies or about land. The usual things. When you have war, then you have plague, and then you have famine, and then you have a city turned to jungle. That's why I don't like to make war – I like to make money.'

Soon they passed beyond the ruins, leaving all signs of human history behind them. Amazon was very aware of the life of the jungle around them. It wasn't quite as noisy as the night jungle, but still barks and roars reached them, sometimes seeming far away, at other times worryingly close.

Under different circumstances she would have loved this adventure, but she couldn't forget the fact that they were being pursued by those who wished them nothing but harm.

It helped them all feel a little more secure that they had the pistol. It was a heavy old Colt 45. Ling-Mei refused to carry it – 'I won't have anything to do with guns,' she'd said. And, of course, no one trusted Chung with the weapon. Frazer would have liked to be in charge of it, but he knew that he was a terrible shot. Amazon was a superb natural shot with a tranquillizer rifle, but she'd never even touched a handgun before. That just left Roger. He switched the safety on and ejected the magazine.

'Five rounds,' he said, and then stuck the pistol in the back of his trousers.

'If we need it, I'll use it,' he added, and Amazon knew that he meant it. But just those five bullets in the clip . . .

Frazer went to the head of the group – partly to get away from Chung, but mainly so he could lead the way with his compass.

'We're still heading north, aren't we, Uncle Roger?' he asked, checking the bearing.

'North it is. But we don't have to be precise. As long as we don't double back, we should hit that river.'

Thirst was their main problem – the forest was drier than the ones Amazon had previously explored in Russia and Canada, and they were all relieved when they found a stream. They fell on their knees and lapped up the water, which was colder and fresher than the muddy mouthfuls they'd swallowed the night before.

'Pity there's no way to sterilize it,' said Ling-Mei, 'but it's better than dying of thirst.'

'Hah,' said Chung, 'that's funny. You die of something much quicker than thirst. Bullet move at about a thousand mile an hour.'

'Put a sock in it, Chung,' said Roger. 'Or head off on your own.'

'Would very much like to, but got to look after Hunts,' he mumbled back.

Roger set a tough pace, but they still had to look for food. Ling-Mei was an expert botanist, and managed to find a few berries to pick and munch as they marched. Amazon and Frazer wolfed them down, but it wasn't enough to satisfy their raging hunger.

Then they hit the jackpot. A group of langurs led them to a big mango tree. Amazon and Frazer climbed up into it and threw down some of the delicious fruit.

From the branches Amazon heard her mother's puzzled exclamation.

'Hey, looks like our daughter has conquered her fear of heights. She's like a monkey up there.'

Amazon threw a mango at her. 'You can't be in TRACKS and be afraid of heights.'

'More to be afraid of than heights,' said Chung, tearing into one of the mangoes, like he hadn't eaten in days.

27

Feline Fury

They walked on into the growing heat of the morning. Clouds of mosquitoes arrived, harried Frazer and then, sated, moved away.

'How far have we covered?' Amazon asked.

Frazer pressed a button. 'Ah, only about eight kilometres.'

'Not enough,' said Ling-Mei, 'not enough. We must go faster.'

Amazon noticed that her father kept pausing and looking behind him.

'Something up, Dad?'

'I've got a feeling we're not alone,' he replied.

'You mean those killers are already on our trail?' said Frazer.

'Not the human killers, no. Something else. Leopard or tiger. You can sense it in the jungle. There's a watchfulness . . .'

They carried on, but each of them now felt the threat from the trees around them. But their spirits were lifted by the light spreading from the east. Each knew that light would bring some protection from the night prowlers – the tigers and leopards. Light also meant that they could move more quickly, and they now upped their pace, jogging for brief periods, then walking again, then moving back to a jog.

And the trees grew ever sparser. That was how Frazer managed to catch his first glimpse. He'd been looking back over his shoulder when he saw the glimmering pattern of light and dark flit between two clumps of vegetation.

'Uncle Roger,' he said urgently, 'it's a tiger, and its right on our tail.'

The group all stopped and Roger went back to investigate.

'Where?'

Roger pointed. The tiger was now quite invisible.

'OK, we keep moving. Tigers don't like to come out of cover. As soon as we get clear of the last of the forest, we'll be fine.'

Now they were all running, aiming for the open spaces ahead of them. But the tiger was keeping pace. Roger stayed at the back – the biggest and therefore the one the tiger was least likely to go for.

They were almost out into the relative safety of the plain when Amazon heard a cry from her father. She looked back, terrified that he'd been attacked by the tiger. However, he'd just fallen, twisting his ankle. They all ran back to him. His face did its best to hide the agony.

Ling-Mei felt his ankle.

'It's a nasty sprain,' she said. 'Can you walk?'

Before he had the chance to answer, they heard a snarl and looked up into the face of a huge Bengal tiger, slowly approaching them. The tiger didn't quite seem to know what to do with this large group. He had planned to swoop on the big one, running at the back. But now this herd had gathered together. Were they dangerous?

The answer was yes. Roger had pulled out the Colt.

The others all froze, except for Chung who yelled out, 'Shoot it! Shoot it!'

No one was quite sure what was going to happen next.

They certainly weren't expecting the tiger to suddenly start running at full pelt away to their right. They spun round to see what it was up to, and then for the first time saw another group of predators that had been lying in wait for them, as two beautiful, sleek lionesses ran to meet the charge of the tiger.

'What's happening, Mum?' asked Amazon.

'Lions and tigers haven't lived together in India for many years. But they're ancient enemies, and won't tolerate each other on their own territory. Any one tiger will usually beat any single lion in a fight, but two against one . . . Who knows?'

The big cats met in a ball of fury, with teeth and claws flashing, ripping, tearing.

'Let's go,' said Ling-Mei, 'before they remember that we're here.'

She tried to help Roger get to his feet, but his foot could not bear any weight and he collapsed with a swallowed groan.

'Go. Leave me. You've got to get to that river. Not just the lions and tiger – the hunters – before they realize we've left the temple area. I can't run on this stupid ankle. There's no option. Just get out of here.'

Amazon let out a wail of despair.

'No, Dad! I've only just found you again. There's no way we're leaving you.'

'Yeah, Uncle Roger,' said Frazer, 'at TRACKS we never leave a foot soldier behind.'

'Look, kids, there's no other way. I can hide out. It'll take them a long time to find me and, before they do, you'll have crossed that river and come back with the police. This way we all win. If I slow you down enough for them to catch us then we all lose.'

The battle between the lions and tiger still raged. The tiger landed a searing blow with its paw, the claws raking along the flank of one of the lionesses. She snarled and twisted away, as the other lioness lunged to her defence, her teeth seeking the tiger's throat. The tiger was too quick, and the teeth snapped at thin air. But now the rest of the pride were coming, and the tiger tried to disengage and

flee back to its refuge in the jungle. Amazon knew that, as soon as the lions had defeated their foe, they would turn their minds to breakfast . . .

And then another voice piped up.

'You Hunts argue like a true family. All very good fun, but we've got work to do. You could say that I owe you a favour. Or you could say that I'm just sick of hearing you yack. Anyway, time to go.'

Then Leopold Chung trotted over to where Roger Hunt was sitting. In one slick move, he swept Roger up and into a fireman's lift, and began to walk swiftly on in the direction of the river.

The others gazed at each other, astonished, then hurried after the pair, leaving the sounds of battling felines behind them.

28

The Pup

Amazon and Frazer simply couldn't believe that their old adversary would do this for them. It was almost as hard to believe that he was even able to. Roger was slender, but he was also tall – he probably weighed 85 kilos. But Chung seemed hardly to notice. His short legs carried him so quickly that the others struggled to keep up.

'I guess we misjudged Mr Chung,' said Frazer.

Amazon looked more sceptical. 'Unless he's up to something devious. You never know with that man.'

Each time they rested, Chung lowered Roger to the floor. And, at each break, Roger argued again that he should be left behind.

'Roger, is this just because you think it's undignified to be carried?' said Ling-Mei, unable to fight the tiny little twitches of laughter at the corners of her mouth.

'Hey,' said Chung, 'it's no shame to be carried by Leopold Chung. I am black belt in kali – Filipino martial art. Also judo, karate, you name it. Don't get to be leader of gang of cut-throats unless you pretty tough guy. OK, off we go again.'

As they marched, the world began to grow gradually lighter around them as the trees thinned. The ground underfoot was now dry and sandy, and they were in much more open countryside, with a few tall trees and clumps of lower bushes and shrubs. They stepped across another narrow stream, which gave them a chance to quench their thirst. Chung got down on his hands and knees and scooped up the water greedily into his mouth, and the others joined him.

Amazon saw another mango tree, with fruit low enough for her to reach up and pluck them. They looked a little unripe, but even a greenish mango was better than nothing.

'No!'

Ling-Mei's voice was close to a screech. Amazon wondered what she'd done wrong.

'*Cerbera odollam*,' said Ling-Mei, slapping the fruit out of her daughter's hand. 'It kills hundreds, maybe thousands in India every year.'

Chung picked up the fruit that Amazon had dropped.

'Ah yeah, we call it suicide tree. Very good if you want to kill someone without getting found out – poison very hard to detect.'

'Chung, you are one creepy guy,' said Frazer.

Chung shrugged, and they walked on, leaving the deadly fruit behind.

Half an hour later, Ling-Mei – who had moved to the front of the group – put up her hand to signal that they should stop.

'Hah,' said Chung, 'lady tired already. Chung can go on, even carrying man on his back.'

'Shut up,' hissed Ling-Mei, crouching down. 'There's something ahead.'

Even as she spoke, Amazon and Frazer heard a sound – a rough squawking and squabbling. Amazon joined Ling-Mei, and she pointed towards a gap in the trees. There was a mob of vultures hopping and flapping around. Whatever it was that they'd been eating, there didn't seem to be much of it left over.

'It should be safe,' said Ling-Mei. 'Those lions must have made the kill. There may be enough left to use to distract the crocodiles in the river.'

Chung stayed with Roger, while the other three approached the vultures. Amazon saw that there were at least three different species – some were brown, some black, all of them had the bald, scrawny neck and that generally scruffy, disreputable look that all vultures have.

'Yuck,' she found herself saying, 'I hate vultures.'

Ling-Mei pointed to one of the birds, which had a few flashes of white among the black feathers.

'That's a white-rumped vulture. Thirty years ago they were the commonest birds of prey in the world.

They were regarded as a pest in India. They lived in the cities, in the countryside, everywhere. Now ninety-nine per cent of them have perished and the species is almost extinct. The same goes for those other vultures out there – the Indian vulture – see that rather handsome grey-backed fellow – and that one with the pink face and red wattles – that's a red-headed vulture.'

'But how? I mean, is someone hunting them?'

'No, it's all to do with a medicine they give to cattle here. The cattle work very hard, and people give them a painkiller to keep them going. The trouble is that the painkiller is lethal to vultures – even in the tiny doses left in the animals' flesh. And, as you know, Hindus won't eat beef, so when the cows die they're just left out in the fields and woods. The vultures eat the cows, and the medicine kills them.'

'That's awful,' said Amazon. She never thought she'd ever feel sorry for a vulture. 'They should ban that stuff.'

'Well, they have, but there's still quite a lot of it in circulation. But the vultures are beginning to make a very slow comeback.'

By now they were quite close, and the vultures began to stretch their wings and flap away. There really wasn't much left to detain them. A few scraps of red-brown fur, some picked-clean bones. Amazon had expected to find one of the Indian species of deer or gazelle, but the carcasses didn't look like that.

'These were dhole . . .' said Ling-Mei, looking at the remains.

'But what kills dhole?' Frazer said. 'I thought even lions and tigers were afraid of them?'

'People do,' said Ling-Mei, crouching down and picking up a bullet casing. 'The hunters must have been out yesterday, having fun. Looks like they killed the whole family. There are lion tracks around, so I guess the pride came along and helped clean up. That must be the dhole den over there.'

She pointed to a low hummock in the ground, with an opening about the right size for a small dog to squeeze through. And at exactly that moment a little face peeped out.

'Oh, is that a pup?' said Amazon.

And almost at once she – and the others – grasped the situation. The whole family – probably eight or ten of them, including some of the bigger pups – had been lured out and massacred. Somehow this little one had escaped. It had been alone and terrified since the day before, and now it was hungry and thirsty.

It looked to Amazon a lot like a fox cub – it had the same long, narrow face and quick, intelligent eyes. Twice it retreated back into the blackness of its den, and twice more it emerged. At last the little creature came scampering out. It shied away from Frazer's outstretched hand and went straight to Amazon.

'Typical,' sniffed Frazer, who was actually a tiny bit jealous of Amazon's way with animals. Big or small, wild or tame, they all seemed to love her.

Amazon let the dhole pup sniff her hand. It made a feeble growling noise, ran halfway back to the den and then came back again. Amazon gently picked it up.

'We can't abandon it,' she said. 'Not if its family has all been killed by those monsters. I'm not leaving it here to starve to death all by itself.'

Ling-Mei looked at her. She knew her daughter well; there was no point arguing about it.

'I know, my darling,' she said softly. 'Come on then – how far to the river, Frazer?'

'If you were right about the original distance then it's about another four kilometres.'

They went back to Roger and Chung. Roger looked at the pup nestled in Amazon's arms, and then at Ling-Mei, and some silent communication passed between them. They both knew that bringing the pup was not a good idea. Chung, however, was not silent.

'Ah, excellent,' he said, 'you brought breakfast.' Then he picked up Roger again and off they went.

29

Another Kill

Amazon put the pup inside her jacket and zipped it up.

'I'm famished,' she said.

'Oh, don't talk about it, Zonnie,' replied Frazer. 'I'm trying real hard not to think about food, but I keep seeing hamburgers and fried eggs and roast chicken floating before me. That's the trouble with eating fruit – it may be good for you, but it doesn't fill you up, no matter how many mangoes you eat.'

'We'll eat all you want when we get out of this,' said Roger Hunt, dangling over Chung's shoulder. 'I'll take you to the best restaurant in London when we're home. You too, Chung.'

'I'll hold you to that,' said Chung.

The land around them had become more arid and brown, but now that they were getting nearer the river a line of green became visible.

'Chung,' said Ling-Mei, 'do you know of any

other defences, apart from the crocs in the river. It seems too . . . easy, somehow.'

'I don't know,' replied Chung. 'I've never been here before. All I've done is send animals, until I make mistake of bringing this boy with the big snake. Chung should have retired from game long ago. But that the trouble with money. You can never have enough. Can never say stop, I don't need another swimming pool. Anyway, if Chung gets out of this place alive, he is changed man.'

Ever since the site of the dhole massacre, they'd been looking for other kills to use to draw away the crocs, and at last they saw the telltale black mass of vultures. This time they were sitting on something more sizeable than a dead wild dog.

'OK, let's get there quickly, before anything nasty turns up.'

They scared the vultures off and found the half-eaten body of a chital – a large Indian deer, speckled with white spots. Like the wild dogs, it had been shot the day before. Unlike the dhole, there was enough left to use as bait.

'Perfect,' said Ling-Mei. 'OK, let's drag this poor old girl down to the river.'

It was one of the most unpleasant things Frazer had ever done. The smell was the worst thing. And the blood and slime from the carcass. It was also, despite being half-eaten, surprisingly heavy. And, even more than heavy, it was an awkward shape.

Amazon wasn't much help as she still cradled the little pup. But they got it back to Chung and Roger, and together they pushed through the trees lining the river.

Before they got to the bank, Ling-Mei told them to stop while she scouted ahead.

'I still don't believe they have no guards other than the crocodiles,' she said. Roger tried to give her the gun, but she shook her head and pulled a face like the one Frazer had worn when smelling the rotten deer.

Frazer, Amazon, Chung and Roger waited for her return by a fallen tree. Now Frazer could see how much the effort of carrying Roger had cost Chung. The morning was still cool, but Chung was drenched in sweat. He looked about ten years older than he had done the day before.

'Will we be safe when we're on the far side, Dad?' asked Amazon.

'Safer,' he replied. 'But we've got to get to a village with a phone. And I don't think Chung will be able to carry me much further. Why don't you two go and see if you can find a couple of forked sticks big and strong enough to serve as crutches. But stay in the treeline – don't show yourselves to anyone waiting out on the far side.'

'Hey,' said Chung, his voice as weak and quavery as an old man's, 'Chung can carry. Chung has debt to pay.'

'Consider it paid, Chung,' replied Roger.

Amazon watched Roger and Chung as they in turn looked at each other. There was something grave and serious in the look, but also something light-hearted. It ended in a smile and a nod.

At that moment Ling-Mei came back.

'I think we could swim it,' she said. 'But it is thick with muggers. And not only muggers. They've got Nile crocodiles there as well. And hippos.'

'Oh sheesh,' said Roger. 'I hate hippos. Those guys are meaner than Kaggs.'

On the Banks

'Is it worth trying to build a raft, Dad?' Amazon suggested. She was thinking in part about the little dhole nestled on her chest. He was going to get awfully wet if they swam across.

'It's tough without rope or twine, or a machete to cut the logs into shape . . .'

'We could probably build a loose raft by weaving thin leafy branches together,' said Ling-Mei. 'I don't know how well it'll hold together, but it might be worth trying.'

They crept carefully down to the riverbank, Roger hobbling as best he could on his improvised crutches. Compared to some of the rivers she'd seen in the Russian Far East and Canada, this one didn't seem too intimidating to Amazon. It was a dull brown colour – almost grey, in fact – reflecting the earth that it moved through. And it had a lazy look to it. It seemed to stroll and amble along, as if it had nowhere special to go.

On the far side she could see more of the same sort of dry, open woodland that they'd been passing through. But, without the extra animals with which the Maharaja had stocked his land, it seemed to hold less of a threat.

Yes, she was sure that if they could only get across then they'd be free and safe.

Then she saw the shapes in the water. She noticed the hippos first – the twitching ears and wide nostrils poking out of the river, then the wide backs breaking the surface.

'Those guys are just about the biggest killers in Africa,' said Frazer. 'Bite a guy right in two.'

'Thanks, Fraze,' said Amazon. 'I really didn't need to hear that.'

'What? Oh yeah, sorry. But don't bother them and they won't bother you. Usually . . .'

And then Amazon saw the longer, narrower shapes in the water.

The crocs.

There were dozens of them. Even more were sunning themselves on the far bank of the river. Amazon thought that she could recognize the two different types, each species sticking with its own kind. One was two or three metres in length, with a broad head. The muggers, she thought. The others were twice the size and exuded menace. Those were the Nile crocodiles.

'At least there aren't any saltwater crocs,' said

Roger, standing close beside her. 'These crocs here are pussycats in comparison.'

He smiled at her and put his arm round her shoulder. 'And I'm not going to let anything happen to my girl, OK?'

Amazon looked back at him and did her best to smile.

Ling-Mei organized the construction of the raft – although 'construction' was too grand a word for it. Amazon sensed how frustrated her mother was getting with the job – they had no tools, except for Frazer's pocketknife, and nothing to tie it together with.

'I'm basically just trying to copy the way a gorilla makes its nest every night,' she said, as she bent and twisted armfuls of foliage together. She did her best to make string from long strips of willow bark, cut away with the knife, but the strips were brittle and kept breaking.

'I hate to rush you, honey,' said Roger, 'but we've got some killers on our tail . . .'

'Fine, fine,' said Ling-Mei, although she was clearly concerned that things were not fine.

Frazer and Amazon looked at the raft. It was little more than a mass of leaves, twigs and branches as big as a bed.

'I don't think it'll take anyone's full weight,' said Ling-Mei, 'but we can hold on and kick for the far side. And, if a hippo attacks, it'll go for the raft and not us. I hope . . .'

Frazer and Ling-Mei dragged the remains of the chital downstream for a hundred metres, and threw it into the water. Then they thrashed at the river with branches. It took the crocs a minute or two to work out what was happening. Then those already in the river angled themselves towards the floating remains, and the ones on the bank scuttled and waddled down to the water, and then, again in their element, beat their tails to take them to the feast.

Ling-Mei and Frazer darted back along the bank.

'It's now or never, guys,' said Ling-Mei. Then she looked at her husband. 'Roger, you ready?' Her voice was tender. 'Your leg?'

'Fine for swimming. When we get to the far side, I can start to worry about it again. But in the water I'm a fish.' Then he turned to his nephew. 'Frazer, you swim, don't you?'

'Of course. Maybe not as good as Amazon, but I can get across that river.'

'Chung?'

'Chung like dolphin.'

'That's not quite what I remember . . .' said Amazon, thinking back to their time as enemies in the South Pacific.

'Doesn't matter,' said Ling-Mei, her voice urgent and almost harsh with authority. 'It looks clear now. No time to waste. In we go. Try not to splash. We'll walk with the raft as far out as we can, then swim along with it. Aim for that fallen tree on the far side. Try to stay together. If anyone gets in trouble, shout to me; the rest go on.' Then she remembered the dhole pup, still nestling inside Amazon's shirt. She knew the futility of trying to persuade her daughter to leave the animal.

'I reckon my raft can carry your pup,' she said.

And so they carried the green and bushy raft into the slow but powerful waters of the river, with the little dhole atop it, like an emperor being carried in a litter.

Amazon and Frazer both felt their nerves jangling, the fear of the pursuit behind now matched by the terror that waited for them in the river.

31

River Tragedy

The still air was furnace-hot now, which made the water in the river surprisingly chilly, and Amazon couldn't help but give a little gasp. But soon it was not the river's temperature but its power that gripped her. The current was strong, and the water soon coursed over their thighs, their waists . . . The bed of the river was slick with mud, and each of them stumbled or slipped. Once Amazon went down on her knees beneath the water, and feared she might be swept away, but her mother and father pulled her up, spluttering. Soon the water was up to their necks and they were floating, kicking out for the far side.

They were no more than a third of the way across when the raft began to disintegrate. The others all began to swim independently, but Amazon kept a tight grip on the section with the dhole pup, which whined and whimpered each time one of its legs broke through the loose weave into the water below.

'Keep together,' cried Ling-Mei again. But it was becoming increasingly hard to swim in the right direction. The current seemed determined to sweep them down towards the crocs, which Amazon knew must by now have finished the remains of the chital and be looking for something more substantial. That knowledge certainly made her kick all the more desperately.

She was halfway. More than halfway. They were going to miss the fallen tree, but that didn't matter – it was the safety of the far bank that counted, not where exactly they landed.

Her mother and father were either side of her, but she could see the pain on Roger's face.

'Mum, help Dad,' she said. 'His ankle . . . he can't really swim. I've got this bit of the raft – it really helps.'

Ling-Mei looked at Roger, just as the current pulled him down and then bobbed him up again. 'I'll be right back,' she said, and kicked towards Roger. At almost the same moment Amazon heard a voice crying out behind her.

She looked back. It was Frazer. He was clearly struggling, splashing in midstream without making any progress. She tried to call out in turn to her mum, but the river swallowed her shouts. She was a stronger swimmer than Frazer, and she should have made sure that he was OK.

She went back, pushing the raft before her, kicking hard against the current to reach him. It seemed to take an age, and her muscles ached. She prayed that she wouldn't get cramp, which would leave her helpless in the water.

'What is it?' she yelled, clinging to his shirt.

'Foot's . . . caught . . .' he gasped back. She could see that he was exhausted from the effort to keep above the water.

'Take your shoe off!'

'Can't. Lace . . . too . . . tight.'

There was nothing for it.

'Give me your knife!'

'What?'

'Now!'

Frazer reached under the water and pulled his pocketknife out.

'You hold the raft,' she said, then took the knife, opened the blade, gulped a lungful of air and went under, still clinging to Frazer's clothing. She tried opening her eyes under the water, but it was pointless – it was thick with silt and she could see nothing. So she felt her way down to the bottom of his leg and found his hiking boot. She pulled and tugged a couple of times, but the whole foot was caught in some sort of root coming up from the river bed. So, with a couple of savage cuts, she sliced through the laces and pulled his foot free.

She came gasping to the surface, expecting to see relief on the face of her cousin.

But that's not what she found. It was something closer to panic. His face was white, his eyes wide, a silent scream frozen on his face. Amazon spun in the water and saw why. Swimming towards them from the direction of the opposite bank was a huge hippo. Its massive jaws were gaping obscenely, its teeth huge brown scimitars.

There was no way they could swim on. She saw

beyond the hippo that her mother and father had reached the far shore. They were now looking back in anguish at her.

Her father had drawn the pistol. Would that work if it had been submerged? She soon found out – he pointed it and fired twice, aiming, Amazon guessed, just in front of the hippo to scare it away.

It had no effect. The hippo was now only a few metres away, its mouth still wide open. Roger aimed again, this time right at the hippo.

And then the mouth crashed closed, not over them, but over . . . what? A log? No – it was a mugger crocodile! The hippo bit down and then threw its head backwards, hurling the three-metre-long reptile high in the air.

Amazon could have laughed. Except that she saw what was happening. The mugger was only the first of many. The allure of the chital had gone, and all the local crocs were now coming back to investigate the new commotion.

'Back,' Amazon shouted at Frazer. 'We've got to get back to the bank.'

Together they swam, each with a hand on the raft – it was now hardly bigger than a dinner plate. Then their feet found the bottom, with the water up around their chins. Amazon looked back behind her and saw to her dismay that two of the colossal Nile crocodiles – each three times as long as an adult human – were surging towards them. They'd never make it to the bank. They were going to be dragged under and killed by the crocs in the notorious death spin, their arms and legs torn off while they still lived.

And then . . .

'Aaaaarghh!'

32

The Unexpected Rescuer

It was Leopold Chung. He appeared as if from nowhere, hurling himself in front of the attacking crocs. He yelled and splashed, and then allowed himself to be carried away downstream with the current, still kicking and thrashing. The nearest of the crocs, as if mesmerized by the performance, swept their long tails back and forth and surged after him.

It gave Frazer and Amazon the few seconds they needed to beat it to the bank, where they dragged themselves from the water, Amazon clutching the pup which, delighted to be off the raft, buried itself in her clothes.

They looked up to see Chung swimming as fast as he could with the crocodiles still in pursuit and closing rapidly. Neither could bear to watch what they knew must happen next. Amazon squeezed her eyes shut as the sound of Chung's cries and splashing faded into the distance.

On the other side of the river Amazon's mother and father stood, helplessly, expressions of utter desolation on their faces. Then Amazon saw Roger very consciously pull himself together, and he shouted across the water:

'The gunshots will have told them that we're here. The hunters, I mean. Go now, as quickly as you can, and find somewhere to hide. Remember everything you've learned. We'll get help and be back as soon as we can. Stay alive. Stay alive.'

Ling-Mei stretched out her hand towards her daughter, almost as if she thought she could reach all the way across the wide river. Then her face crumpled and she turned away. In another moment they were gone, heading into the long grasses, Roger leaning heavily on his wife and still hobbling badly.

Amazon could not believe that she was losing her parents again. But she also felt the will to live well up inside her. She was not going to let these monstrous people destroy her family. Nor did she intend to let them slaughter the beautiful and precious animals in the reserve. She and Frazer were going to stay alive.

And then she thought of Chung.

'Do you think he stands a chance?'

Frazer shook his head. But then, thinking that he had to be positive, he shrugged. 'You never know. He's always seemed like a lucky guy. But I'll tell you what, that debt is paid. He's a brave man.'

'Come on,' Amazon said, wiping away a tear that might have been for Chung. 'We've got to move.'

Frazer nodded. He only had one boot, but he didn't complain, and they began to jog along the bank of the river, staying within the shelter offered by the trees.

'We don't know if that guy told them that we were in the temple complex, but if he did they'll have got there early this morning and found us gone. So that means we know they'll be coming from that direction –' He pointed the way they'd travelled that morning. 'All we've got to do is keep moving. If we can stay out of their sight for the next few hours, your mum and dad should be able to get a message to the authorities. So I say we track along the river, and try to stick to any wooded or jungly areas we come across. This place is huge and, unless they have dogs, they'll never find us.'

And at exactly that moment they heard, far off, the faint baying of hounds.

'Oh nuts,' said Frazer.

33

Swallowed!

It was proving to be a very tricky time for the giant python. The man she had caught and squeezed until he should have been dead had refused to die. She had found that out when she had temporarily released him because of the attentions of a family of warthogs, which had happened to blunder her way. The mother warthog, assuming that the snake was a threat, had charged her repeatedly, jabbing those tusks maddeningly into her ribs.

When the warthog finally decided that enough was enough, the snake tried to begin her feast, only to discover that dinner had recovered enough to stagger away. She pursued him for a while, but it was no use – even a half-strangled human can outrun a python.

Her neck was bruised and her scales dented, the damage caused by the gorilla now added to by the slashing of the warthog, but her hunger was undimmed. And now she sensed the vibration on the forest floor. It drew her, the way the scent of decay draws flies.

Again she sensed several humans. They were gathered round a dead fire, and they were talking. Of course she couldn't know that this was the team of hunters on the trail of the Hunts. They had found the scout, half mad with pain and thirst and terror. He had pointed them to the temples, and they'd come to pick up the trail.

She also sensed the yapping and baying of dogs.

The snake couldn't feel the anger and frustration in the group. But she did sense it when two of them moved away.

She followed them. One was almost as big as the gorilla. The other was smaller. They stood a little apart, making water.

This was too easy. She reared up and hurled herself at the smaller man's head, her mouth closing most of the way round it. And the coils enwrapped him. He was dead in a minute.

The strange thing was the behaviour of the other man. He just stood and watched, a grim smile on his face. Until, that is, the killing had been done and the snake began to swallow her prey. Then the man began to shout, and the others came running. The man who had first stood by, passively, now kicked her in the stomach, and the others yelled and screamed. The dogs were around her, snapping. One man fired a gun wildly into the shadows.

This was highly stressful to the snake, and so she regurgitated the body, vomiting it up with a coating of slime. And then she was away, angrier and hungrier than ever.

And the pale German, Herr Frapp, was dead.

34

The River Run

There is nothing, Frazer found out, that speeds you up like the knowledge that you're being hunted with dogs. He cursed his rotten luck in losing that boot. The ground was hard and dry, and he kept standing on rocks and roots and thorns, and soon his foot was bruised and bleeding.

'Got to stop, Zonnie,' he said. 'Got to sort my foot out.'

Amazon looked at the foot and had a think.

'Nasty,' she said. 'OK, take off your boot and sock from the left foot and put the sock on your right foot.'

'What? Oh, double up the sock on my bad foot, you mean? Good idea.'

Then Amazon took her own shoes and socks off and gave both the socks to Frazer. 'Put these on the bad foot, too.'

Frazer just about managed to get all the socks on – it looked most peculiar. So now he had a damp boot and no sock on his left foot, and four pairs of wet socks on his right.

He stood up and tried it out.

'It's a little better,' he conceded. 'But, if we weren't about to get killed, I'd say this was darned funny.'

And then he and Amazon, exhausted, hunted, terrified, began to laugh. But their laughter was quickly silenced when they heard the howling and barking of the hounds once more. The baying was still distant, but definitely nearer. The little pup inside Amazon's shirt whimpered at the sound.

'You good to go?' Amazon said to Frazer.

'I'll race you,' he smiled back. And off they went again.

They were two fit young people, light on their feet, and they knew how to run. It certainly helped that the past few months had been full of intense physical challenges: it meant that they were both at their absolute athletic peak.

The most awkward thing for Amazon was running with the dhole pup. She tried shifting it in various ways, but in the end just ran with it under her arm. It didn't seem to mind, but just hung limply, like a toy animal. Amazon suspected that dholes were the sort of creatures that often changed their dens, and so the pups had to get used to being carried around.

They followed the river for an hour, covering a good five kilometres, thinking of nothing more than staying out of the range of the hunters' guns, and stopping only to gulp water from some of the small streams that fed the river. The sun was not yet at its zenith, but it was still hot, and the shade of the trees was almost as welcome as the cover they afforded.

Another time, and in different circumstances, they would both have loved this place. Monkeys – langurs and macaques – leapt above them in the trees. Unseen deer and antelope bounded noisily away as their pounding feet approached; beautiful and gaudy birds flew with iridescent bursts of colour across the river.

Then, through a gap in the trees, they saw looming up before them the great wall of the hunting estate, topped by the ugly new metal of the electric fence. It was still a couple of kilometres away, but its size, even at that distance, was truly daunting.

'Is there any point us even trying to climb over that thing?' asked Amazon, as they got their breath back.

Frazer looked at the wall, his eyes straining to see if there were any hope of scaling its smooth, sheer face.

He shook his head. 'Even if we could climb it – which we can't – we'd be sitting ducks to those hunters. They'd just pick us off. We've got to keep under cover. I think we're better off trying the river again.'

They still hadn't left the strip of forest that clung

to the river, and it only took them a minute to make their way to the bank. If they were hoping to find the river free from danger, they were sorely disappointed. The brown water was alive with the long, low, drifting shapes of muggers and Nile crocs. And, even if they'd wanted to run the gauntlet of the crocs, they'd have had to get through the hippos that wallowed in the muddy shallows near the bank.

They turned away from the river and checked the other side, where the trees gave way to the dusty plain. It was very exposed. There were just a few bushes and isolated trees, and then, in the distance, the jungle area surrounding the temple complex.

And they also saw an approaching dust cloud that could only mean one thing.

'It's them, isn't it?' said Amazon. 'The hunters and the dogs . . .'

Frazer set his mouth in a hard line. 'We're staying alive, Zonnie,' he said. 'I want to see Kaggs jailed. I want to see all of them jailed. I want them rotting in some Indian prison until they're bald and toothless old men.'

Then he considered their options again.

'OK, we can't get across the river. We can't get over the wall. We can't go across the plain – if the hunters don't get us, the lions will. But look – this line of trees here turns off before it reaches the wall.

It looks to me like it may eventually reach back to the jungle – or at least part of the way there. It's our only chance. Let's get going.'

Amazon nodded back at Frazer. At that moment she couldn't help thinking how proud she was to be his cousin. He had one boot and a bloody foot, but he wasn't giving in. And neither was she.

35

Kaggs Perplexed

Merlin Kaggs was now in a foul mood, even by his own grim standards. He looked at the frayed ends of the ropes. The hounds had been useful. They had tracked the blasted Hunt mob from the temple complex down to the river. There he had looked into the brown water, alive with crocs and hippos, and seen that nobody could possibly hope to get across. And, anyway, the dogs had strained at the leash, pulling away along the bank.

And then the ropes, held by the trackers, had snapped. That should not have happened. Had someone failed to check them properly before they set out? If so, there would be a price to pay. Or could someone have deliberately sabotaged them? If so, who and why? Anyway, the dogs had gone. They might stay on the trail for a while, but then they'd head back to the lodge, assuming the leopards, tigers and lions didn't get them.

And then he heard a scream, back at the river.

Tutting and grumbling, he ran back. That stupid fat Texan, Laramie, had somehow fallen in the river. The big African was reaching out, trying to pull him in, but the Texan couldn't haul his bulk out of the water. And there, coming at them like torpedoes, were three crocs.

Kaggs made a quick calculation. It was better to lose one more customer rather than two. He stepped towards Amunda Banda, as if he were going to help him pull the Texan in. Then he simply brought his arm up, breaking the grip that the chief had on Laramie's collar.

'Leave it, chief,' he said, and dragged him away. Behind them the screams of the Texan lasted only as long as it took for the crocs to take him under.

'You're a bad man, Mr Kaggs,' said Banda, giving Kaggs a long, intense stare, his face unreadable.

'Takes one to know one,' replied Kaggs, a grim smile on his face.

Just at that moment one of the Indian scouts bent down to study the ground. He shouted something in Hindi and pointed towards the west, signalling that he'd found a bootprint pointing in that direction.

'Well, what are we waiting for?' Kaggs yelled to the hunters. 'Let's ride.'

36

Stalked

Frazer was right. The strip of woodland that lined the river curved away before it reached the wall and carried on until it joined with the jungle at the heart of the hunting estate. It had obviously been designed to provide a corridor for the jungle animals to go down to the river, without having to cross the plain.

It wasn't much of a plan – following the trees back to the temple – but it was better than nothing, and the cousins ran on with renewed energy. It gave them both a certain grim satisfaction that the hunters – who had expected to find them as sitting ducks in the temple – were being led a merry dance.

But there was something that niggled at both of them, just below the level of consciousness. This strip of woodland was eerily quiet. That sense of life all around them – even though much of it had been heard rather than seen – was lacking here. Once or twice, Amazon thought she saw something from the corner of her eye. A movement perhaps or a splash of deeper darkness against the dappled shadows. But when she looked again it would just be the breeze passing across the leaves, or sunlight playing through the undergrowth.

And then Amazon thought that the pup was becoming restless. It wriggled and yelped, and seemed to want . . . something.

'Are you thirsty, little guy?' she said to him. And putting it into words made her realize how thirsty *she* was. 'We need some water,' she said to Frazer.

'I don't want to go back to the river . . .' he replied. 'It'll mean we fall right into their hands. Next stream we come to.'

It wasn't long before they found a meagre trickle of water making its way across the forest floor. Amazon knelt and cupped her hand to it, and tried to offer the water to the baby dhole. But the little animal wriggled and yelped even more, until Amazon could barely hold it. And then she noticed that Frazer was looking not at her and the dhole, but into the trees, and his face was etched with lines of worry. He put his hand to his pocket and took out the pocketknife, and flicked open the biggest blade. It was almost comically small.

'What is it, Fraze?' she asked. 'The hunters?'

'Not the hunters,' he said, without looking at her. 'The hunter. The *ultimate* hunter.'

'The tiger? It's back?'

'No, not a tiger. It's a black panther. A big one.

And when a leopard – which is what the panther
is – turns rogue, there's nothing to touch it for killing
ability.'

And then Amazon, following his eyes, saw it too.
Somehow the earlier encounter with the tiger had
left her unafraid. But that was because her mother
and father were there, and her father had a gun. But
now they were just two children alone.

With a pocketknife.

The big male panther was ten metres away. He'd

been stalking them as they ran through the woodland. Now he knew that he'd been seen and so he was reappraising his options.

'Hold my hand,' said Frazer. 'We've got to make sure we stay close together. It'll probably try to separate us . . .'

Amazon stood up and took Frazer's outstretched hand, still holding the squirming pup in the other.

'Now, slowly, back off.'

They edged away. As they did so, the panther stepped forward, keeping the same distance between them. His ears were twisted so that the backs were facing them, showing a paler spot on the black background, and his tail moved rigidly from side to side. Both Frazer and Amazon knew exactly what this meant: the panther was about to attack.

37

Unexpected Help

'Trees . . . climb . . .' hissed Amazon, her fear at the stalking panther stripping her of all eloquence.

'No. Leopards are as happy as monkeys in trees,' Frazer whispered back. 'There's only one thing for it. We have to prove to it that we're not prey. We have to show it who's boss.'

'And how the h-heck do we do that?'

'We charge it, screaming and yelling at the tops of our voices.'

'Will it work?'

Frazer looked at his cousin. The old smile was playing at the corners of his mouth.

'Let's find out. On three. One . . . two . . .'

But, before Frazer reached three, they heard a sound behind them. It was a combination of barking, yickering, snarling and a bizarre sort of whistle. At the same moment the panther's body language was transformed. His ears were now flat against his skull, and his face wore what could only be described as a grimace. He was showing his teeth, but it almost seemed to be a submissive grin, rather than an aggressive snarl.

Most importantly, it was the panther now that was backing away.

'What the . . .?' said Frazer, looking behind him. And there he saw something at the same time beautiful and mesmerizing and frightening. Flowing like water, leaping, bounding, scampering, came a pack of dholes. He tried to count them, but got lost somewhere around ten – it was almost impossible to keep track of them, so quickly did they move.

Just before they reached them, the pack split into two. Half flowed on towards the panther, which was clearly highly alarmed. The dholes were fearless, diving straight into the attack. They snapped and nipped at the great black cat, more than three times the weight of any individual dhole. The panther responded by trying to swipe them with his razor-sharp claws. But the dholes were just so nimble and, each time that destruction seemed imminent, they would dive back, or dip under, or jump over the blow.

It was an amazing spectacle, intense and exciting, but Amazon and Frazer were not able to enjoy it. The other half of the dhole pack – six of the wild dogs, each the size of a Labrador, but with more fox-like features – gathered in a semi-circle round the two children. It was a very different sort of approach to the one that they used with the panther.

Rather than the quicksilver, darting attacks, they were almost motionless, but were staring intently at Frazer and Amazon, teeth bared, tongues lolling.

'It's the puppy,' said Frazer, suddenly understanding what this was all about. 'The whole pack can't have been destroyed. These were probably out hunting when the rest of them were shot. Put the pup down and let's get away . . .'

Very slowly, Amazon put the young dhole down on the ground. Immediately it hurled itself towards one of the adults, yelping out its joy. It leapt up and licked the face of what Amazon knew must be its mother. She smiled in joyous relief – this had vindicated all her efforts in keeping the little creature alive.

The mother picked up the baby in her mouth, with great tenderness, and slipped away into the woods.

Both Amazon and Frazer expected the dholes still facing them to either follow the mother or to join in with the harrying of the panther – which had itself retreated out of sight, although they could still hear that the attack was in full swing. But they didn't. The snarling, threatening look of the dogs had not gone away with the recovery of the pup. They pressed forward a little more, making the children edge backwards again.

'What are they doing, Fraze? They've got what they want, haven't they?'

'I don't know, Zonnie – I've never heard of dhole attacking people before. But maybe they think we had something to do with the annihilation of the others, back at the den. Or maybe . . . maybe they're just . . . hungry.'

That was a truly horrifying thought. Frazer had heard all about how dholes killed their prey. Lacking the killer bite of a big cat, or even a larger member of the dog family, like the wolf, they tended to take their kills apart piece by piece.

Again he scanned the area. He saw through the trees behind them some kind of structure – obviously man-made, but more than that he couldn't say. He hadn't realized that they'd already got back as far as the temple complex, but he couldn't think what else it might be.

'Zonnie, there's one of the temple buildings about two hundred metres behind us. If we can climb on top of it, we might stand a chance . . . You ready to run?'

Amazon nodded, unable to take her eyes off the dholes.

'If you trip or fall, or if they somehow get you on the ground, you have to fight your way up. Understand?'

Again she nodded. She knew what it would mean to fall beneath the teeth of the compact killers.

'But I won't leave you, don't worry. OK, where did I get up to before on my counting?'

'Three.'

'GO!'

And the children spun and raced away, terror giving their feet wings.

Instantly they heard the yickering and whistling and the pattering of light feet after them.

Amazon made it fifty metres before she felt the first nip. The dhole bit her just behind the knee. Its sharp teeth tore through the tough fabric of her combat trousers as if it were tissue paper. It was lucky that the teeth didn't sink into her flesh, but merely scraped across her skin. For a second she nearly lost her footing, as the terror at being harried threatened to overwhelm her, but she managed to stay upright and hurtle on towards the building before them. It was enough to give her another burst of adrenalin, and she shot ahead of Frazer. And, as she did, she saw, through an obscuring screen of trees, what they were heading towards.

It didn't look much like a temple.

Still she dared not slow down. She looked back over her shoulder. Poor Frazer, his foot draped now in the last ragged bits of torn sock, was slowing down. Three dhole were running close to him, snapping at his legs. They couldn't go on much longer. They had to –

And then Amazon felt an almighty crunch and the world went black.

38

The Refuge

Frazer, running just behind Amazon, saw it happen. She had run smack into an armed guard, sending them both reeling to the ground. The guard had been smoking a cigarette and listening to an iPod. That was why he had missed the approaching racket.

Behind him was the building that Frazer had at first mistaken for a temple ruin. But this was no ruin: it was a long, low concrete block. There was a steel door left ajar – obviously the guard had just emerged from this.

The wild dogs were still all around them, snapping and snarling.

Frazer barely paused as he pulled Amazon up by the arm. Then in the same movement he swooped again to grab the AK-47 the guard had dropped. The guard looked at them, dazed and perplexed, and then at the dogs, his eyes suddenly wide with terror. Amazon and Frazer raced quickly to the open door, passed through and slammed it shut before the guard reached it. They heard his agonized slapping at the hard metal, and then the shouts, diminishing as he fled through the forest.

'Should we have . . .?' wondered Amazon aloud, thinking of the danger the guard was in.

'It's life and death here, Zonnie,' replied Frazer. 'And remember we're the good guys.'

'What is this place?' Amazon asked, looking around.

They were in a grey utility room full of junk – buckets and ladders and empty boxes. A single bare bulb dangled from a wire in the ceiling. There was another door at the back of the room.

'Dunno,' replied Frazer. 'But I say we go explore.' He was still holding the AK-47.

'Do you know how to use that thing?' Amazon asked, wondering what might lie ahead of them.

'Nope. And it doesn't matter. I don't plan on shooting anyone. But it might come in handy, if we have to do any . . . *persuading*. Come on.'

He opened the second door carefully and stuck his nose through. Beyond it was a passageway, as characterless and functional as a corridor in a hospital, or a morgue.

'I've got a funny feeling about this,' said Amazon. 'I don't . . . I don't like it.'

'Well, I didn't much like it out there with the tigers, wild dogs and murderous hunters. We may be able to find somewhere to hide in here. Or maybe even a phone. It all looks kind of modern, so they must have telecoms . . .'

They crept along the corridor, lit with a flickering fluorescent light that gave them both a sickly pallor. Frazer now felt that same sense of veiled dread as Amazon. And then they both stopped dead in their tracks, frozen by a sound that echoed along the corridor, but yet seemed to come from all around them. It was a long, low moan, somehow both human and bestial. Instinctively the cousins drew close together. Frazer clutched the gun, his finger reaching for the trigger.

'What was that?' asked Amazon, although she was really speaking to herself.

Frazer just shook his head. 'Do you want to go back?' he added a moment later.

Amazon thought for a second and then said, 'No,' decisively. 'You're right. Back there, we're doomed. This way there's at least some hope.'

They passed through another door, and found themselves in a slightly lighter corridor. It was newly painted and the lights at least weren't flickering.

'I've a feeling we came in the back door,' said Frazer. 'That's why it was all shabby. Whatever this place is, the business end is up ahead somewhere.'

They came to a third door. This one was very different. It was made of shining steel, with a small window cut in it. Frazer signalled for Amazon to crouch down.

'I have no idea what this place is for, but my guess is that this is where the action is . . .'

'I think I know,' said Amazon. 'Drexler said something about his research. That was why he got involved in all this.'

'Research? What kind of research? I mean, he had all the facilities he needed back at TRACKS. Why would he have to keep it all secret? Why don't you have a sneaky peak through the window and see what you can see?'

Amazon slowly stood up so she could look through the little round window. There was a spacious room beyond, with a number of wooden lab benches. In one corner there was a large stainless-steel drum, with a heavy lid, locked shut with clamps. In another corner was a white plastic device the size of a washing machine, with a clear glass lid. Laptops were open on the benches, and there was a large microscope and other bits of technical equipment that Amazon thought she half recognized from the science block back at school or from TV documentaries.

There were two people inside the lab, both dressed in white coats. One had his back to Amazon, but she could see the other quite well – he was an Indian with thick spectacles and a thin moustache. As Amazon looked on, weirdly fascinated, he moved over to the steel drum. He put on a pair of surgical gloves and opened a lid, which released a fog of cold air. Then, using a pair of tongs, he lifted out a metal tube. He carried this back to a bench, unscrewed the top and, again using the tongs, removed a test tube.

At that moment the other scientist in the room turned round. Chance had it that he faced directly towards the door. Amazon realized that he could see her, and their eyes met for a moment. He raised an eyebrow quizzically. And then Dr Drexler started to move towards a large red button on the wall.

39

The Lab

There was no time for Amazon to explain to Frazer what she was doing. She had maybe three seconds to reach Drexler before he set off the alarm. She pulled open the door, knocking Frazer – who'd been crouched behind it – sprawling backwards. Then she tore across the hard floor of the lab and hurled herself at Drexler's outstretched arm.

She reached it just before his jabbing finger hit the button.

All she had done, however, was to delay the inevitable. She tried to cling to his arm, but, ultimately, he was a grown man and she was still just a thirteen-year-old girl. He shook her free.

The other scientist had also recovered from his initial astonishment and was moving towards her. Once again, Dr Drexler prepared to press the alarm.

'Touch that and you lose your hand.'

Frazer was pointing the AK-47 at Drexler's arm. Drexler, whose face had been utterly emotionless as he grappled with Amazon, suddenly smiled. It was a wooden, false sort of a smile, but a smile nevertheless.

'My dear boy,' he said, 'we both know that you couldn't hit my hand if you had a dozen shots.'

'I reckon you're right, Doc,' replied Frazer, wearing a smile that, in contrast to Drexler's, was most definitely genuine. 'I'm just as likely to accidentally shoot you in the head as the hand . . .'

Drexler's false smile vanished and he edged away from the button.

'I really am delighted to see you two young people,' he said, his voice struggling to remain calm and even.

'Can it, Drexler,' replied Frazer. 'Don't even pretend that you didn't know what this was all about. You knew that we were toast.' Then he turned to Amazon. 'Zonnie, use the phone to call the police – you dial 100 in India. Drexler – you move and I'm going to shoot you in the legs – and, as we've already established that I'm a terrible shot, I just can't say what I might hit.'

Drexler was still playing it cool. 'I'm afraid,' he said, his voice mild, 'that there's no contact at all with the outside world from this facility – that phone only connects to the main lodge. And all internet traffic is routed through there, too. There's no way to get a message in or out. Mr Kaggs is somewhat . . . *paranoid*.'

The shot, in the confines of the lab, was deafening,

and Amazon couldn't help but cringe down in fear. Luckily the bullet lodged itself in the wall behind Drexler, rather than ricocheting round the room.

The gun was still smoking in Frazer's hands.

What nobody else knew was that it was an accident – Frazer hadn't meant to pull the trigger. But now that he'd done it, and seen the effect it had had, he was happy to use it to his advantage.

'You're a liar. It's what you are, and all you do is lie. You've betrayed us all just to cook up some nutty scheme. Mad scientists are meant to be interesting. But you, you're boring. I don't believe there's no way to get a message out. And, I'll tell you what, I'm not going to start shooting you or your friend Igor here, I'm going to start shooting up these wacky experiments.'

Then Frazer aimed the assault rifle at one of the pieces of equipment – the plastic box with the clear lid. The effect on the usually icy Drexler was instantaneous. With a cry of agony, he hurled himself in between Frazer and the equipment.

'Noooooo!' he screamed. 'You don't know what you're doing!'

'Now *thaaaaaaat's* a bit more like it,' said Frazer, smiling coldly at Drexler's reaction. 'A slice of authentic fruitcake from the mad prof.'

Amazon was less amused and more intrigued.

'OK, Drexler,' she said, keeping her voice calm. 'Why don't you tell us exactly what this is all about, before my hot-headed cousin accidentally turns everything in here into a hi-tech colander.'

Drexler licked his dry lips with a thin tongue.

'I . . . I tried to explain a little of this to you before. You know, I suppose, about the research that has been undertaken with animal cloning?'

Even Frazer was getting interested now. 'Er, you mean when they make, like, a sheep from another sheep, and they're identical?'

'Yes, that's one thing they can do. But perhaps you also saw that movie about the possibility of cloning dinosaurs.'

'Yeah, that was pretty cool!'

'And impossible! To clone an animal, you need to get all or most of the DNA from the cell nucleus. It's our DNA, as you know, that makes us what we are. It's the blueprint from which we are created. And each tiny cell nucleus contains about two metres of it – if it were untangled and stretched out. It's incredibly fragile and delicate. Fossilization completely destroys DNA. But, if an animal were frozen, even for thousands of years . . . well then, that's a different matter.'

Amazon and Frazer looked at each other, both trying to take in what Drexler was saying. Then an idea began to form in Amazon's mind. She remembered Drexler's slightly odd behaviour in the Russian Far East when they'd been there. There was talk of him having undertaken some mission further north. She scanned her memories for news stories that she had heard or seen. And the image of something very large loomed up in her mind. But Drexler was still speaking.

'The problem was always that, when a cell freezes, ice crystals form inside its structures, and these tear the cell apart and rupture the nucleus. And it's the devil's own work to get two metres of genetic material back into the nucleus. It would be like trying to fit, say, a giant reticulated python into your pocket, young man.'

Drexler emitted one of his dry, humourless laughs, the sound echoing round the room.

'But then we found that brain cells survive the freezing process a little better than other cells. They have a higher content of glucose, which seems to afford them some protection. Nevertheless, the path was long and arduous. The nucleus had to be extracted from the rest of the brain cell. Then we had to find a donor egg, in which we could implant the brain nucleus. Nothing seemed to work. The obvious donor species – a very close relative of the original, extinct animal – proved to be just a little too different, and each of the attempts failed.

'Then we were lucky. We found a frozen specimen with intact eggs in her ovaries. The DNA in the egg nucleus was not well preserved, but we had the brain nucleus from another animal. So we simply implanted it into an egg of the same extinct species.

Such a breakthrough! This new egg could then be persuaded to begin the process of cell division that leads, ultimately, to a baby, a new creature, not seen on earth for ten thousand years.'

As Drexler was speaking, Frazer was aware that his assistant was inching towards him. It was obvious what he was about to do and, when he made his move, Frazer was ready for him.

It wasn't, despite the difference in their ages, a fair fight. The scientist, although a much older man, was used to wielding nothing more than a pipette and a Bunsen burner, whereas Frazer had spent his whole life being active in the great outdoors, not to mention being a black belt in tae kwon do. Plus, he had an AK-47 assault rifle in his hands, which he used to clout the man on the side of the head, sending him spinning to the ground.

'Oh, Samit,' said Drexler to the dazed and uncomprehending scientist, 'there was really no need for that. I want to show these young people what we've achieved. I think they'll understand the importance of our work, see that it has to go on . . .'

And then Drexler moved to the second door in the lab – the one that led to the rest of the complex. As he opened it, two things flowed in: the sound and the smell. Amazon and Frazer followed him out, and found themselves in yet another corridor. There were doors to the left and right, but Drexler hurried along on his thin legs, so that Frazer and Amazon had to jog to keep up.

'Slow down, Drexler,' said Frazer, but the man ignored him, and Frazer realized his only options were to follow along or shoot him in the back.

All the time the smell – rich, heavy, stifling – and the sounds – snorts, snuffles, occasional wilder noises, almost like the sound of screeching tyres on a car taking a corner too fast – grew.

And then Drexler burst through a door at the far end of the corridor, just as Frazer caught up with him, and the three of them – Samit, still lying on the floor, stunned, had not followed – were in a huge cavernous space, divided by a narrow metal walkway, that was the continuation of the corridor. They moved forward a little distance along the walkway. Ten metres below them was a sight to fill any human heart with delight, amazement and wonder.

40

The Hairy Truth!

'MAMMOTHS!' said Amazon, her mouth, her eyes, her whole mind wide with astonishment.

And there they were below them, twelve woolly mammoths. There were mothers with tiny calves, one big bull, its horns curving like immense scythes, and a smattering of adolescents, looking bored and irritable. All had the characteristic high-domed heads and small ears that Amazon had seen in illustrations. They were covered in coarse hair, most a rich ruddy-brown, but some a lovely pale honey colour, and others were almost black.

As well as the mammoths, there was one elderly female Asian elephant. As soon as the old elephant saw Drexler up on the walkway, she became agitated and trumpeted several times. She paced about below them, reaching up with her trunk.

'That's old Ellie,' said Drexler, an odd smile on his face. 'She was the original surrogate mother, fifteen years ago. Without her parenting skills, none

of this would have been possible. But I'm sad to say that she resents me somewhat. I had to take away a few of her babies for further experimentation and study. I dread to think what would happen if she managed to get that trunk round me . . .'

Drexler turned to face Frazer and Amazon. There was a pleading look in his eyes all of a sudden, an expression Amazon would never have expected from the scientist. 'So, now you see why I had to do what I did. Your father, Frazer, forbade research of this nature. His opinion was that all of the resources of

TRACKS should go into protecting living species. He didn't have the imagination to see what could be done, the intelligence to understand the implications.'

'Well, what the heck are you going to do with them? Release them into the wild? Sell them to zoos?' asked Frazer, still gawping at the mammoths.

'My goal is to one day repopulate the Siberian steppe with these great creatures. But yes, our research must still be funded, so we have to examine all possibilities for raising finance . . .'

And then Amazon understood. 'That man . . . Kaggs . . . he's going to sell the right to shoot these creatures, isn't he?'

Drexler jutted out his chin. 'Not for many years. This breeding herd is far too valuable for that. Millions of dollars have been invested, tens of millions. They must be preserved at all costs. Mr Kaggs and the Maharaja both know that. Perhaps, at some stage, superfluous animals, excess bulls that would otherwise fight among themselves . . . well, they might be, ah, disposed of . . . One cannot be sentimental about these things when the greater good is at stake. Our eyes must be on the ultimate prize; we –'

'Oh, shut up, you bozo,' said Frazer, his voice dripping with scorn and disgust. 'I always thought you were a creep. Bringing these magnificent creatures back from the dead just to kill them again . . . you're nuts, and we're going to stop you. I'm gonna personally –'

Amazon interrupted him. 'Fraze, what's that other guy doing, Samit . . .?'

'Well, I gave him a good old whack on the head . . .' But then Frazer remembered the phone with its link back to the lodge. He also remembered that there was a gang of proven killers on their trail.

'Hold this,' he said, giving the gun to Amazon. 'You're a better shot than I am. Blast his toes off if he gives you any trouble.'

Amazon didn't want to take the gun, but she couldn't see what the alternative was. Frazer disappeared back through the door towards the lab. Then Drexler spoke to her.

'You're not going to shoot me, are you, Amazon? Apart from anything else, a bullet from an AK-47 at this distance would pass straight through my body and could easily go on to kill one of those baby mammoths down there. You wouldn't want that, would you?'

And, without another word, Drexler turned and fled along the walkway. He was absolutely right: Amazon could never hurt a living creature, even one as despicable as Drexler. She considered firing into the air, but didn't want to frighten the mammoths.

So she let him go.

At the far end there was a metal stairway, down

which Drexler half ran, half fell. He was among the mammoths for no more than a couple of seconds, but it was long enough for old Ellie to come charging towards him, trumpeting her rage. For a moment Amazon thought that the elephant was going to catch Drexler, but then he opened a narrow door, set into a much bigger set of doors at the back of the mammoth enclosure, and was out into the daylight. Ellie crashed against the door just as it slammed shut.

41

Surrounded!

Amazon ran back to the lab. She found Frazer using the telephone cord – ripped from the wall – to tie Samit to a chair.

'It really wasn't a fair fight,' he said, smiling. 'But he'd already got a call in to the lodge. Where's Drexler . . .?'

'He ran. I couldn't . . .'

Frazer nodded. 'Of course not. Nor could I. Anyway, we've got bigger problems than that scumbag. Take a look at this.'

He pointed to one of the laptops. It had been set up as a monitor for CCTV pictures from the outside. There were two different views on the screen. One showed the back of the complex, from which direction they'd come. It was a chilling sight.

There were at least a dozen armed guards in khaki uniforms there. The other view was of the front of the place – Amazon realized it must be the way out that Drexler had taken. That is where the hunters were gathered, along with the Maharaja and Kaggs.

One thing that Amazon did notice was that not all the hunters were present. She couldn't see the German, Herr Frapp, or the fat Texan, Laramie. As well as being reduced in number, they also looked ragged and worn, as if they'd endured a lot.

But now they were here. And they were armed. They looked like they were going to war. Each was draped in weapons – rifles, pistols, machine guns. Big Zee, the gangster, had what looked an awful lot like a bazooka.

'This is it, isn't it?' said Amazon, half to Frazer, half to herself.

Frazer's face was set hard.

'Maybe. Maybe not. But, whatever happens, I'm taking some of those killers down with me. It's blaze of glory time, Zonnie.'

Then, as they watched, Kaggs came forward. He was carrying a megaphone. He started to speak. The CCTV camera must have had a microphone, because the voice came through on the laptop's little speaker.

'We know you're in there, Roger old friend. And your lovely, lovely wife. And those two nice little kids. You've done well. Provided good sport. In fact, such good sport that we're prepared to call it a day. The boys here think they've got value for money. We can kiss and make up. What do you say?'

There was a pause, and Amazon saw Kaggs joke with the hunters. Then he turned back to face them again, his face cracking up with laughter.

'No, no, of course you don't believe me. We know each other too well. You're going to die. And that witch of a wife of yours too. But here's the deal, and you have my word, and the word of the Maharaja here, who's a decent sort of a chap, as you know. Come out and we'll spare the children. They'll be kept here safe on the estate. We can't allow them ever to be set free, of course, but the Maharaja will make sure that they're looked after as well as any English country gent might care for his guests.

'There you go. That's the deal. You've got ten minutes to decide. Then we come in and massacre you all. And it won't be quick, I promise you. Ten minutes. Then we're coming.'

Frazer picked up the laptop and threw it against the wall, quite close to the cringing Samit.

'They still think my mum and dad are with us,' said Amazon. 'That's something. They probably think we've got more guns than we have. They're scared to come in. Maybe we can hold out until help arrives?'

'I've got a better idea,' said Frazer. 'You, Samit, those big doors at the front – how do they open? Lie to me and I'll feed you to the mammoths.'

'They're opened electrically, from a console on the wall.'

Then Frazer grinned and said to Amazon, 'Ever take a ride on an elephant?'

42

The Hunters Wait

The mighty doors of the mammoth enclosure began to slide open.

Kaggs was not expecting this.

The whole manhunt business had proved to be something of a disaster. Luckily the dead men had paid him well in advance, but he doubted that the survivors would go back home praising the fun adventure holiday they'd enjoyed. And word of mouth was so important in enterprises of this kind.

Back to the original plan – big-game hunting, rare animals and then, the cherry on the cake, mammoths! Who could resist the idea of putting a large-calibre bullet in the brain of a creature like that! Not yet, though. Like that bore Drexler kept saying, they had to build up the herd. Just a little further down the line they'd be a cash crop.

But now those big doors were easing open. He'd thought that either there would be no reply from the wretched Hunt family, which would mean they'd have to go in there and work through the place, room by room. Or perhaps that old fool would really send the kids out. Well, Merlin Kaggs wasn't known as the sort of idiot who left witnesses to his crimes, no sir.

'OK, boys,' he said to the remaining killers. He studied them closely. Leconte, the Frenchman, looked like the sort that would have pulled the wings off butterflies for fun, as a kid; Big Zee, the absurd gangster with his gold teeth and gold chains and gold-plated bazooka. That buffoon, Smethwyck, who expected someone to put the toothpaste on his toothbrush every morning. But McKlintock, the Australian media baron, he was a steely one. Ice water in his veins. The Maharaja looked nervous. It was probably time to get rid of him, maybe install some other puppet in his place.

And then there was Drexler. The most boring man he'd ever met. He'd run out of the lab building, blabbing like a madman, and Kaggs had had him dragged back out of the way. Didn't want a jabbering fool like that messing up the last stages of the hunt. But then, without his mega-brain, they'd never have got the mammoths. And, without his treachery, they'd never have got some of those other animals too. So he was a necessary evil. For now.

Last of all there was that African. Hardly said

a word, but looked as if he could crush your skull like an eggshell. Corrupt as hell, of course, but Kaggs liked a man who could be bought.

'Get ready. They might go for glory and try to rush us.'

There was the sound of guns being cocked. They were ready to unleash a hail of lead that would take out an army.

43

The Charge of the Heavy Brigade

Amazon's answer to Frazer's question about ever having ridden on an elephant was, of course, no, and now she wasn't sure that she'd ever want to do it again. She held tightly on to Frazer, who seemed as happy up there as if he were sitting on a sofa, watching the TV.

It had been surprisingly easy to get on the elephant's back. Clearly the old girl had spent a long time as a tame elephant, probably working timber camps in India. So, with a few gentle words from Frazer, she'd knelt before them, providing a handy knee for them to clamber up. And the gentleness of old Ellie seemed to permeate the whole small herd, even the rambunctious juvenile bulls. Ellie held them all in complete sway. Even though some of the others towered over her, she was still the matriarch of the herd, the leader, the guide.

The mammoths clustered round her, their trunks reaching up to touch and sniff at Amazon and Frazer.

It was like something from a dream. It should have been a nightmare – they were surrounded by giant shaggy monsters – but their gentleness and curiosity swept away Amazon's fears.

'Are we really going to do this?' she asked Frazer.

'We are, cuz. It's death or glory. And me, I prefer glory, so those guys out there had better watch out.'

The dilemma for Frazer had been how to get the mammoths to charge. He was gambling on two things – the first was that they'd follow old Ellie. The second . . . well, the second he was about to find out.

He nudged the old elephant towards the wall and hit the button with the butt of his gun. There was a crank and a grind, and very slowly the doors began to swing open – they were wide enough to drive a big truck through.

And, just as Frazer had hoped, he saw – or rather felt – Ellie grow tense. She raised her trunk and sniffed the air. She had caught the scent of the hated Drexler. She began to pace back and forth in that fast walk that in the elephant kind passes for a run. She put her shoulder to the great iron door to speed its progress.

Harsh light from the blue sky poured in, dazzling Frazer and Amazon. They could not see, for a second, what was outside. It didn't matter. Frazer knew that surprise was everything. He dug his heels into Ellie and yelled at the top of his voice, and then fired off a quick burst from the AK-47, which sounded in the enclosed space like a rolling peal of thunder.

And then Ellie, with Frazer and Amazon on her back, became thunder herself. She charged from the enclosure, and suddenly she was a young elephant again.

A young elephant in a murderous mood.

Now that his eyes were used to the light, Frazer looked ahead. And what he saw dismayed him. He had hoped that the sight of a herd of charging mammoths might make the hunters panic and break. But there they still stood in a neat line, their heavy weapons trained on the elephant and her riders.

Frazer strained to look back over his shoulder. And he despaired. The door had become jammed somehow, and there was only enough of a gap to let out one beast at a time. And because they were all trying to get through, it meant that none could.

They were on their own.

There was no giant hairy backup.

A withering hail of bullets was going to cut them down before they came close to reaching their killers.

Frazer gritted his teeth. There was no turning back now. They were going to ride on into legend.

Ahead of him he saw the unmistakable hunched figure of Kaggs, his craggy face beginning to split into a grin.

And then he saw something else. Something strange. The huge African – he couldn't remember

the man's name – dropped his own weapon, a long-barrelled rifle with a telescopic sight, and turned to the hunter next to him – the Englishman, Smethwyck – and pulled the shotgun out of his hand and hurled it away. Smethwyck's face was almost comically baffled. Then the African picked him up as easily as if he were a child, held him high above his head and hurled him into the bushes.

Frazer just could not understand what was happening. It was simply inexplicable . . .

But it didn't stop. Next the African – Amunda Banda, yes, that was his name – produced a savage, downward swinging punch that landed at the base of the gangster Big Zee's neck. He fell to his knees and, as he did so, he accidentally discharged his bazooka, which blasted into the gates behind Frazer.

Frazer looked back and saw that it had blown one of the gates off its hinges. Suddenly the mammoths were out, and their pent-up fury sent them charging after the matriarch. Frazer faced forward again and saw the hunters, and the guards with them, looking dismayed, terrified, astounded. Their line became ragged. They turned and began to flee.

Kaggs alone stood still. He raised a machine gun to his shoulder and aimed it at the face of the elephant. Before he could pull the trigger the African was on him. They wrestled for control of the gun, and Frazer heard a short burst. He saw the flowing garment that the African wore billow out and then a red stain spread across it.

Kaggs had the gun again, but now it was too late for him. The mammoths were upon him. He fled with the others, trying to find refuge from those massive trampling feet among the trees.

Ellie was not concerned with Kaggs. She was looking for Drexler. And there he was, running away on his long legs.

Then Frazer, whose heart had almost burst with adrenalin-fuelled joy at their victory, saw something that made him groan in despair. A line of big trucks was coming towards them. Reinforcements, he knew, from the Maharaja's private army. This fight was not over. This fight had barely begun.

44

Reunions

Things now became utterly chaotic. The mammoths charged hither and thither, and it was hard to know if they were simply exultant at their freedom, or enraged at their former captors. Random shots rang out, hitting nothing. Drexler still ran towards the oncoming trucks, seeking salvation and safety there. Ellie, who most certainly *was* enraged, thundered after him, with Amazon and Frazer still clinging to her mighty back.

Amazon didn't know what to think. Should she be elated or distraught? Stuck behind Frazer, she couldn't properly see what was going on. There was dust everywhere, and the noise was deafening. Screams, shots, trumpeting. The rumbling of the trucks.

The trucks began to pull up and fan out across the track. Drexler had almost reached them when he stopped dead. Frazer wondered if they could still escape, riding the elephant out into the jungle. He dug his left heel into her side, which should have got her to turn that way . . . But Ellie was too intent on her prize. She carried on towards Drexler and the trucks. Trucks that were now disgorging their passengers. And yes, there were guards in khaki uniforms. And others. Civilians.

Amazon peered over Frazer's shoulder, and tried to wipe the sweat and dust from her eyes.

It.

Couldn't.

Be.

There, striding forward, was the solid, muscular form of her Uncle Hal. And behind him came her mother and father, who was leaning heavily on a serious-looking Bluey.

And, at the back, Miranda Coverdale.

Amazon felt a huge pang of guilt for leaping to the conclusion that Miranda was the traitor.

And, last of all, Mehmet. Somehow he must have got through.

The guards weren't guards at all. They were Indian policemen and women. Although, faced with the sight of stampeding prehistoric animals, most were hastily climbing back into their vehicles.

Amazon couldn't blame them – the sight of fifteen woolly mammoths and one very annoyed she-elephant rampaging before them must have been quite something to behold.

Even the Hunts were flabbergasted – but their

children were there and so they had no intention of running.

The first to reach them was Drexler, his clothes ragged and torn, his face a mask of terror. He threw himself at the feet of Hal Hunt and begged, 'Save me, save me.'

Hal looked up at the approaching elephant – which had, in fact, slowed down. But it was Roger Hunt who came forward and spoke – not to Frazer or Amazon, but to the elephant.

'Hey, old girl,' he said in a clear voice, 'good to see you again after all these years. You remember me, don't you?'

And Ellie, who had been rampant with rage, stopped, stretched out her trunk and sniffed at the face of Roger Hunt, and then knelt down and allowed the children to scramble from her back, while Roger stroked her old head.

'We were friends a long time ago,' said Roger to the gawping watchers around him, 'back when we were kids, and collected animals for zoos. I'd recognize Ellie anywhere. She used to carry me and a very mean sloth bear around on her back . . . I knew she was here, but that was when we thought the Maharaja was running a game reserve and not a slaughterhouse.'

'Get in the back of the car,' said Hal Hunt to the cringing Drexler, 'before I let this elephant turn you into chicken-liver pâté.'

Drexler did as he was told. The Indian police officers had, by this stage, regained their nerve and begun to spread out, picking up the surviving hunters.

The mammoths had lost interest in charging about, causing mayhem. This was their first taste of freedom and they had some exploring to do.

'Mammoths . . .?' said Ling-Mei, looking for the first time, in Amazon's experience, totally perplexed. 'How? Why?'

'It's a long story, Mum,' said Amazon. 'And at last we've got the time to tell it. But how did you find us?'

'It was Mehmet,' said Hal Hunt. 'He made it to the police. Must have had a heck of a job getting his meaning across, but luckily I'd used my contacts to get the word out that you were missing, and they must have put two and two together. We found your mother and father lost as usual in the woods across the river. Lucky Roger here had Ling-Mei with him – he never did learn a blasted thing about surviving in the wild. He'd have been tiger food without her.'

'Brother,' said Roger, smiling, 'if my ankle was up to it, I'd kick your ass. But I might just get my daughter to do it for me.'

'And she could too,' chipped in Frazer, which brought a peal of laughter from them all. And then the Hunts – Frazer and Amazon, Hal and Roger and Ling-Mei – came together in what might just have been the greatest, longest, most heart-felt group hug in the history of the world.

And then Amazon drew back from the hug, a look of sadness on her face.

'Chung,' she said. 'He saved us . . .'

'Oh,' said Hal, 'it would take more than crocs and hippos to finish that rascal off. He was picked up further down the river. He's recovering in hospital. He's looking at some serious jail time. Unless he happens to slip away, which, frankly, I wouldn't put past him.'

And then Frazer remembered something important.

'Dad, there was a guy, an African guy . . . when we first came out, it was just us – I mean me and Zonnie and the elephant – and they were all there waiting. They would have cut us to ribbons. But this African guy started fighting them – he took the guns off them . . . he totally saved our lives. But Kaggs shot him before he ran off.'

'Take us to him,' said Hal. Frazer led the way to where he'd last seen the African.

He was lying on his back, looking up with open eyes into the pure blue of the sky. For a moment Frazer thought that he was dead. And then the eyes blinked and he looked towards them as they came, and at the same time a half-smile appeared on his lips, and Hal Hunt yelled out a name.

'Joro!'

Roger looked stunned for a second. Then he slapped his head. 'Of course! How could I have forgotten?'

Then the two older Hunts ran to the man's side. Roger cradled his head, while Hal held his hand. Someone brought over a medical kit, and Ling-Mei staunched the bleeding as best she could.

'What's going on?' asked Amazon, utterly mystified.

Her father looked up at her.

'Many years ago this man acted as our guide in Africa. He . . . well, he had to stand up against some pretty tough enemies, and he had to make some hard decisions about right and wrong. I knew that he'd gone on to be a leader of his people, but I just didn't recognize him.'

'But I,' said Joro, his laughter turning into a bubbling cough, 'recognized *you*. I was aware that this man Kaggs and his slaves were taking animals from my country. I was retired from politics, and I wanted one more challenge. So I came here to discover and expose the truth. When I saw what was happening, I still had to keep quiet and wait for the time to strike.'

'You saved us, Mr Joro,' said Amazon. She could see that the front of his robe was red and sticky.

'Hold on,' said Hal. 'We can get an air ambulance here, and you'll be in hospital in no time.'

'Don't worry, my brother,' replied Joro. 'I am not ready yet to die. There are too many stories for us all to tell, the young and the old alike.'

And each of the figures gathered there thought that there was much truth in this, and they began to tell the stories, until the throbbing sound of the rotor blades of the approaching air ambulance drowned them out.

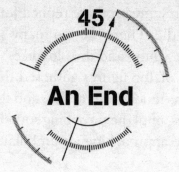

45

An End

The snake had been drawn by the vibrations. She was now very hungry indeed. The recent disappointments festered in her.

She saw the man. He was drenched in sweat that smelled strong and sweet to her. His chest was heaving and his face contorted with exhaustion, fear and hatred. She advanced upon him rapidly, her hunger meaning that she moved with less caution than usual.

And so Merlin Kaggs was alerted by the rustle of leaves on the dry ground. Without wasting time by looking to see what was coming, he pulled the pistol from the holster at his side.

It was too late. The huge mouth of the snake was already closing over his face. He managed to fire off one, two, three wild shots, which were heard by other jungle creatures – the dhole in their den, the stalking leopard, the sulking tiger, the chattering monkeys, and by the lions out on the plain.

And then Merlin Kaggs was silenced.

TOP 10 FACTS:
RETICULATED PYTHONS

1. **RETICULATED PYTHONS** are the world's longest snakes. They can grow around ten metres in length. Female reticulated pythons are usually larger than the males.

2. The word 'reticulation' means squares and lines that create a distinctive net-like pattern. **RETICULATED PYTHONS** get their name from their scales, which show a characteristic diamond and crisscrossed-line pattern.

3. **RETICULATED PYTHONS** live in humid, tropical climates in South-east Asia where there's lots of rainfall. For this reason they like to come out at night when the air is moister. In the daytime they like to find a damp spot in which to hide.

4. Most snakes lay eggs, and **PYTHONS** have been known to lay more than a hundred eggs at a time!

5. A snake's scales are made of keratin, which is the same material as your fingernails! So even though their skin is flexible, it's quite hard and tough too.

6. **PYTHONS** don't kill their prey using venom. They suffocate their victim by wrapping themselves round its body, waiting for it to breathe out and then gripping even tighter.

7. **RETICULATED PYTHONS** are ambush hunters, mainly preying on mammals. It can take several weeks for them to digest large prey, such as a pig or antelope.

8. The average lifespan for a **RETICULATED PYTHON** in captivity is between twenty-one to twenty-five years.

9. **RETICULATED PYTHONS** are hunted for their skins and many thousands are killed every year. As a result, numbers of this species of snake in the wild are diminishing.

10. The Latin name for a reticulated python is **PYTHON RETICULATUS**.

It all started with a Scarecrow

Puffin is over seventy years old.
Sounds ancient, doesn't it? But Puffin has never been
so lively. We're always on the lookout for the next big
idea, which is how it began all those years ago.

Penguin Books was a big idea from the mind of
a man called Allen Lane, who in 1935 invented
the quality paperback and changed the world.
**And from great Penguins, great Puffins grew,
changing the face of children's books forever.**

The first four Puffin Picture Books were hatched in 1940 and the
first Puffin story book featured a man with broomstick arms called
Worzel Gummidge. In 1967 Kaye Webb, Puffin Editor, started the
Puffin Club, promising to 'make children into readers'.
She kept that promise and over 200,000 children became devoted
Puffineers through their quarterly instalments of *Puffin Post*.

Many years from now, we hope you'll look back and
remember Puffin with a smile. **No matter what your age
or what you're into, there's a Puffin for everyone.**
The possibilities are endless, but one thing is for sure:
whether it's a picture book or a paperback, a sticker book
or a hardback, **if it's got that little Puffin
on it – it's bound to be good.**